MW00939221
tiger
Haven
ARIEL MARIE

Cover Design by Desiree DeOrto

Edited by: Dana Hook at Rebel Edit & Design

Interior Book Design by Ashley Michel of AM Creations

This is a work of fiction. Names, characters, organizations, businesses, events, and incidents are a figment of the author's imagination and are used fictitiously. Any similarities to real people, businesses, locations, history, and events are a coincidence.

A Note From The Author

WARNING: Due to the explicit language and graphic sexual scenes, this book is intended for mature (18 years +) readers only. If things of this nature offend you, this book would not be for you. If you like a good action story with hot steamy scenes with tiger shifters, then you have chosen wisely…

~Ariel Marie

ONE

"There are many threats to animals in the wild," Dr. Charlee Black announced to her young freshman biology class.

She took in the lecture hall that was crammed with an estimated three hundred students and smiled. She loved educating young minds who were open to learn. It was a challenge, but well worth it to Charlee. These students were like putty in her hands, they just needed to be molded. Her freshman lecture was always packed and would have a wait list to get in it.

"There are different levels to the threats that animals face. The ones that most concern scientists today are those that fit the criteria of endangered, critically endangered, and extinct in the wild." She turned to the screen on the wall as she pointed her remote to the projector and clicked the button for her next slide.

"Dr. Black, what about those that are extinct?" a young man asked with his hand raised in the middle of the lecture hall.

"That's a good question." She nodded, enjoying how engaged her class was. "But, unfortunately, when an animal has reached that phase, we're too late. No animal can come back from extinction."

Silence greeted her answer. It was hard to imagine a species no longer existing in the wild, and only existing in history books. This was reality. Plenty of animals were now extinct who many scientists tried to save, but to no avail. The species' disappeared.

"But that's where you come in, right, Dr. Black?" Jenny asked.

"Well, yes," Charlee replied. She could tell that Jenny was bright and very interested in the field. The semester was only a third of the way through, and Jenny had made a few appointments with her as questions arose.

Her heart skipped a beat just thinking of her research and the upcoming field assignment she would embark upon. Her life's work as a Wildlife Biologist had led her all over the globe. She was an expert Mammologist, with her primary focus on the Amur tigers.

"Outside of teaching, you're trying to save certain animals, right? To keep them from becoming extinct?" Jenny continued. "Isn't that hard if mankind doesn't want to cooperate?"

"Exactly!" Charlee exclaimed, a huge grin spreading across her face. "And that will take me into my next slide, Jenny. Thank you."

She continued her lecture, going in to how humans play a vital role in saving wildlife. With all the destruction of rainforests, and the millions of acres of forests used for man, animals in the wild were suffering. Charlee hoped and prayed that if she could educate at least one person about the dangers of animals going extinct, it could change the world. She believed that it would only take one person to hear her lecture, to be inspired to change the world.

"Michael will cover my freshman lectures while I'm gone," Charlee informed her secretary, Ellen. "For my sophomore classes, it will be Jim, and Brian will cover my junior and senior classes."

"And your emails?" Ellen asked, scribbling in her notebook while Charlee rummaged around her office, trying to decide what to take with her on her trip.

It had been almost a year since Charlee had been on a field assignment, and she was excited. The past year had been spent in her lab, doing speaking engagements around the world and teaching at the local university. She had made a name for herself, and as one of the top senior species experts on tigers, it left her very little time to have a personal life. But lately, she was feeling like a caged animal, needing to break free. This trip was just what she needed.

She would be traveling with a team to Far East Russia, to an area known as the Four Corners. It was a mountainous region that bordered Russia, China, Mongolia, and Kazakhstan. Charlee had received a call from the Russian government asking for her expertise to help secure the natural tiger habitat of the Four Corners.

"I'll leave the emails to be forwarded to you, and then you can disperse them as you see fit. You would know best who to distribute them to. I should only be gone a month, so hopefully, there won't be too much to worry about while I'm gone."

Charlee didn't know what she would do without Ellen. Her secretary was a middle-aged woman who ran the office with an iron fist.

"Don't worry, Dr. Black," Ellen said. With a warm smile, she stood from her seat. Charlee blew out a sigh of relief. Of course, as she should have known, Ellen would take care of the office. "I'll handle everything. They won't even know that you're gone."

"I'm sure you will," Charlee advised. Walking over to Ellen, she gave her a tight hug." I just wish I could take you with me."

"Me? In the rainforest? Ha!" Ellen laughed, patting her perfectly coifed graying hair. "Me and humidity do not get along."

Charlee chuckled as she watched her secretary leave the room. She glanced around her large office, taking in the overpacked bookcases, souvenirs, and artifacts she had collected over the years. Pride filled her chest as she took in her prized possessions. She had made a name for herself all right.

At the young age of thirty-four, it was unheard of for a woman to accomplish so much in her field. But Charlee had busted her ass all her life to get to where she was. She graduated from high school at the young age of sixteen. While most girls her age were learning how to drive and going to homecoming dances, Charlee was already enrolled at the local university. By seventeen, she had published her first article in a distinguished journal that got

her recognized as one of the youngest, most brilliant minds of the future.

"Dr. Black, Ms. Benton is on the line for you. Do you want to take it? Or shall I take a message? Ellen's voice floated through the air over the phone's intercom.

"I'll take it," Charlee replied, picking up her phone.

"Very well," Ellen said. "Ms. Benton, Dr. Black is on the line. Have a wonderful evening."

"Hey, Char!" Malena's perky voice came through the line.

"What's up, Malena?" Charlee settled into her plush leather chair at her desk.

"How's the packing?"

"Oh, you know me. Just getting started," Charlee chuckled. "I'm a little rusty with the packing part of a trip, but you know, it's like riding a bike. You never forget."

"No, I don't remember hearing anyone compare packing for an expedition to riding a bike," Malena giggled. "Do I need to come over and help you?"

"No, I got it. I think with all my degrees, I can handle packing," Charlee laughed, kicking her heels off underneath her desk. "I know you weren't calling me about packing. What's up?"

"Well, sheesh. You would think a gal could call her BFF and chat a second before getting down to business," Malena snorted.

"I'm sorry," Charlee groaned. "I'm stressing about handing over my classes to the guys and making sure I have everything handled before we leave."

Malena and Charlee had been best friends since undergraduate school. They had met their freshman year by getting assigned as roommates. It was a perfect match from day one. They had both majored in biology, completing undergrad school together, and even got their master's degrees together. Charlee went on to get her post-doctorate degree and soon brought her best friend in as her assistant once she had secured a position at her current university.

"You won't have anything to worry about. Your classes will be in great hands, and you know Ellen will have that office taken care of. Matter of fact, I'll bet money that your office will be cleaned and catalogued better than how you left it when you come back."

Charlee looked around her office and knew that Malena was right. Ellen had a special knack for cleaning that bordered along the lines of OCD.

"You're right," she sighed into the phone as she rested her feet on her desk. She adjusted her skirt and prayed no one walked into her office, or they would catch an eye full.

"Anyhow, I called about some news I received that I thought I would share with you. There's one special interest group that I hear will be traveling to the same region that we're set to observe."

"You have got to be shitting me," Charlee gasped. She knew that when special interest groups got involved, things could become a mess. Certain groups believed that money and time were wasted on saving animals, and that their efforts would be better served going toward human causes.

"Well, this one is apparently on our side. It's a privately funded organization that has a special interest in tigers and preserving their natural habitat."

"Really? Which one?" Charlee's brain started running a mile a minute at the possibility of connecting with a well-known group for donations. Yes, her job was rewarding, but if she was to accomplish anything, she would need money, and lots of it. And that was where the private sector always came in. They loved to donate big money in order to say that they helped changed the world.

"An organization called SPAT."

"SPAT?" Charlee echoed. She was familiar with most of the larger wildlife conservation groups, but this one, she'd never heard of.

"The Society for the Protection of Amur Tigers," Malena read off. "I've been researching them, and they're a very privately funded group. It's headed up by a guy named Weston Rogavac. I looked him up, and he looks to be some wealthy guy who tries to stay out of the limelight. Most times, when his organization donates money to any fund, they do it anonymously."

"Well, if they're on our side and going to the same region, I think I need to introduce myself."

"You may want to do more than introduce yourself." Malena laughed.

"What does that mean?" she asked, pulling the hair pins from her hair to free the thick, dark mass, which fell to her shoulders in waves. It was after hours and time for her to relax.

"Pull him up on your computer," Malena suggested with a giggle.

Charlee dropped her feet to the floor while reaching for her mouse. She shook it to wake her computer up as she rolled her eyes at her friend.

"Does this really matter?" Charlee muttered, typing his name into the internet search bar. "I just need a few minutes of his time to get him to donate money to our research."

"I think you may want more than a few minutes of Mr. Weston Rogavac's time." Malena's voice dropped low with a seductive chuckle.

"Really, Malena? At a time like this—" Charlee's voice caught in her throat as the image of one Weston Rogavac appeared on her screen.

Holy mother of God.

His dark eyes bored into hers from the computer screen. His strong jawline was covered in a five o'clock shadow that gave him a rugged look, even though he was in a perfectly tailored suit.

"Cat got the professor's tongue?" Malena's voice broke through Charlee's lust filled fog.

"Huh? I mean…yes, he's good looking, but you know I don't have time for love," Charlee stammered, unable to take her eyes off his picture.

"Who said anything about love? We're going to be in the heat and humidity of Russia for a month. Haven't you heard the saying, 'What happens in the rainforest, stays in the rainforest?'"

TWO

It's rare that a group of tigers would band together. In the wild, a tiger was known to be a solitary animal. But in the shifter world, it was quite common for the tiger shifters of the world to work together for the goodness of their wild counterparts. That was where SPAT came in. The Society for the Protection of Amur Tigers was an organization that was funded and ran by shifters.

The shifter world was a secret society that humans weren't aware of, and that's the way shifters liked it. Humans would not be able to handle the fact that they were not the only ones living on Earth.

"Have a good evening, Mr. Rogavac," the doorman, Jeffrey, called out as he held the door open for West.

"Have a good night, Jeffrey. Check at the desk, I left you a little gift." West smiled as he walked to the waiting dark sedan.

"Thank you, sir!" Jeffrey called out behind him. West knew that tomorrow was Jeffrey's birthday, and was an avid fan of the Cleveland Cavaliers. So West took it upon himself to leave two floor side tickets to tomorrow's game for the doorman.

Weston Rogavac may have grown up wealthy beyond anyone's imagination, but he had always remained grounded. "Treat your employees as you would want to be treated, and they will be loyal forever" was drilled into his head by his late father, Novak Rogavac.

"Mr. Rogavac," his driver Mason greeted him.

"Evening, Mason." West nodded to his driver as he unbuttoned his suit jacket before settling into the plush, luxury sedan. The shutting of the door cut off the noise from the street, leaving him in a comforting silence.

West glanced up at the building that his family built from he ground up. His family's building was located in the heart of downtown Cleveland. The building stretched high into the clouds, with Rogavac Industries plastered across the front of

it. Pride filled his chest as he thought of what the building stood for. The Rogavac family was one of the wealthiest shifter families in the world.

Rogavac Industries was the powerhouse in the biomedical engineering field, with their hands in all the latest medical technologies. His company was involved in many projects that would change the future of medicine, everything from advanced medical machines for physicians to diagnose the latest diseases, to designing state-of-the-art artificial limbs. Their latest advancement would be announced—the first artificial kidney—within the next year or so.

His family's name would go down in the history books, but as a human owned company. The general public would know of their work and accomplishments, but never know that it was shifters who developed the technology.

"Home, sir?" Mason's deep voice floated through the partition.

"No, take me to The Deck," West instructed, speaking of the trendy bar that he had begun to favor recently. It was located on the bank of the Flats, an up-and-coming area in Cleveland, located on Lake Erie. "I'm meeting Luka for drinks tonight."

"Yes, sir."

Luka Batalo and West had been friends since they were cubs; their families longtime friends. It was only natural that both tiger cubs would grow up and stay close friends. In college, West studied business at one of the most lucrative schools in the country, while Luka studied biomedical engineering. It was a no-brainer for Luka to come work for West.

The sound of a phone ringing gained West's attention from the passing city scenery. He pulled his cell phone from his inner jacket pocket and checked the screen.

His mother.

"Evening, Mother," West answered.

"Why so formal, Weston?" the musical voice of his mother, Inez Rogavac, came across the line.

"No reason. Just now leaving the office," he replied, a small smile appearing on his face. He rubbed his jaw and winced from the stubble that covered his skin.

"You sound tired. Don't be out too late. Your plane leaves early in the morning," Inez reminded him. He smirked, thinking that no matter how old he was, she would always try to mother him.

"I'll be fine, Mom," he chuckled. "Luka and I are just stopping for drinks and to discuss a little informal SPAT business.

"Well, you know how you boys are." His mother laughed. "The city better watch out if Luka Batalo and Weston Rogavac are hitting the town."

"I promise not to get into too much trouble tonight," he promised, knowing that Inez Rogavac

was the only woman in the world that had him wrapped around her little finger.

It really wasn't a bad idea. His tiger sat up a little at the thought of finding a beautiful woman tonight and taking her home with him.

Not a bad idea at all.

"It's about time you showed up," Luka said, standing from his chair in their private VIP section of the nightclub. Luka stood at the same height as West, at six foot three. With his dark blond hair and amber eyes, few would know he was a tiger shifter.

"Well, some of us don't get to play in the lab." West smiled as reached his longtime friend. He slapped him on the back and gestured for him to sit back down. "Some of us have to play adult and meet with board members that keep our company afloat," he joked, taking his own seat.

"Hi, handsome." A soft voice appeared at his side. The waitress was dressed in the standard uniform of the nightclub—a low-cut shirt and tight jeans that looked as if she had to be poured into them. She was pretty, but did nothing for him or his tiger. "What can I get you?"

He knew that his mother was right about him and Luka, and decided to play it safe. "I'll take a Godfather," he answered, turning back to his friend.

"Good choice! I'll take one too," Luka said with a devilish smile before he turned back to West. "So, are you ready for the trip tomorrow?"

"Of course. You sound just like my mother," West mumbled as he turned to stare at the patrons of the club. It was a Friday evening, and he knew that the normal crowd would be showing up soon. This was one of the more popular places for the over thirty crowd, and would soon be packed.

"Mother knows best," Luka joked, tossing a balled-up napkin his way.

"Fuck off." West laughed. "So what information have you gathered about our trip?" he asked, switching to business. SPAT meant everything to him, and if traveling around the world to help with one of the largest natural habitats was the plan, so be it.

As a member of the most prominent tiger shifter family, it was his duty to help see that their wild counterparts survived.

"We're headed to the Four Corners," Luka drawled, switching over to business as well. He reached over to the empty chair next to him and pulled some papers from his briefcase, then handed a few to West. "The Russian government is calling in

leading experts to help with preserving the rainforest and mountainous regions of Far East Russia."

"Siberia?"

"Yes, the motherland," Luka noted with a nod of his head.

West's tiger began to pace beneath his skin. His animal would have a field day running through the mountains with other tigers.

"Who are the experts that they called in?" West asked, browsing through the papers.

"All the usual ones, but I found it interesting that this time, they've called in Dr. Charlee Black from Eastern State University as the senior species specialist."

West's ears instantly perked up at the mention of Dr. Black. He had certainly heard of her. She was a well-known wildlife biologist who was sought after for many speaking engagements, and for her research regarding the Amur tigers.

Just thinking of the good doctor had his tiger purring. Yes, he knew exactly who she was. His organization had donated plenty of money to her research foundation under the disguise of another organization. She was a brilliant scientist that had most certainly captured his tiger's attention. Her image was burned into his memory. Her curvy frame, and that thick, dark hair. His fingers craved to pull it in the heat of passion. Her slightly slanted eyes captivated him in every picture he had seen of her.

"Dr. Black's team will be leaving tomorrow as well." Luka's voice broke through West's thoughts. He shifted slightly, trying to adjust his hardening cock, hoping that his friend hadn't caught on that he was attracted to the doctor. Very much attracted to her. What West found crazy was that he had this reaction just by thinking of her. What the hell would his body do when they finally met?

"Here you go," the waitress announced, gently placing their drinks down in front of them on napkins.

"Thank you, pretty lady," Luka said with a wide smile. West held back a roll of his eyes.

"Can I interest you gentlemen in a little food?" she asked with a flirtatious smile. She tucked her hair behind an ear as she focused her gaze on Luka.

"Sure, why not?" Luka laughed, rattling off his order. They had both been to this bar so many times, they each had the menu memorized.

"What about security?" West asked after he placed his order. He repeated himself again to get Luka's attention, who was staring off after the waitress.

"The Russian government has agreed to provide security for the trip."

"Good. I wouldn't want any of the poachers interfering with the mission. It's too important." West took a sip of his drink as his thoughts turned to the trip. Should they really trust the Russian government?

Fuck no.

"Call in Drago. Make sure that he comes. I want him and his men on this trip." West turned back to Luka.

"It's last minute, but I'm sure he'll come," Luka said.

The main reason that SPAT would be there was because of the increase in poaching. Someone had to deal with the illegal poachers. The government always stated that their hands were full, or that they never found any traces of the murderers. West and his people would go and handle the poachers. They didn't need any assistance from the government to handle them. They would take matters into their own hands.

"Well, I say we finish this business discussion tomorrow on our very long plane ride and take advantage of the lovely ladies in this club." Luka motioned with his glass to the throng of women standing by the bar.

West barked out a laugh at his friend and shut the file. He was right. They had a long flight ahead of them, and would have plenty of time on his private

jet to discuss business. He would be flying off to the other side of the world tomorrow. Tonight, he could take the time to relax with his friend and enjoy his evening.

THREE

"Oh my goodness! I forgot how muggy it can be on this side of the world," Malena groaned, wiping the sweat from her brow.

"We've been out of the airport for all of two minutes." Charlee laughed at her friend's overly dramatic complaint. She stretched her arms in the air for a brief second. She had to admit, it did feel good to finally be able to walk around and not be on an airplane. The time difference would definitely throw her off for a day or so before her body would adjust. It was nighttime when they left the United States, and now it was evening where they were. Her internal clock would catch up after a good night's rest.

They would be meeting up with the other scientist that would be arriving soon.

Alf Jenson was a student that won the honor of coming along on this once-in-a-lifetime trip with her. He was the top student in her graduate level biological science course.

"Rest well on the plane, Alf?" she called out from her position as he stepped out of the automatic doors of the small airport terminal.

"I did, Professor. Thanks," he replied with a grin as he joined Jim York, their animal ecologist, and Alton Cummings, the team's senior researcher.

"Oh, to be young again," Charlee chuckled as she glanced around, finding the other team members hovered near their cab. Everyone would have severe jet lag if she went by the yawns echoing throughout the air.

The drivers were currently loading the bags into the back of their passenger vans. The team had a two-hour drive ahead of them to get to their first destination, the small town of Lyrino, Russia. There, they would stay at a lodge until the other team arrived. Charlee couldn't wait. This would be a historic mission for her, working with some of the other infamous biologists and scientists who would all play a vital role in preserving this habitat.

"Well, you better stretch your legs a little longer because according to the itinerary, we have a two-hour drive," Charlee informed Malena, looking down at her phone.

"I hope this lodge is like one of those vacation bed and breakfast—"

"Who are you, and what have you done with my assistant?" Charlee asked with a straight face.

She shook her head at her best friend's wistfulness, but silently, she too hoped that it would be a nice place to stay. Once they hit their final destination—in the wild—it would be days, if not weeks before they returned to a warm, comfortable bed.

"A girl can dream, can't she?" Malena joked.

"Whatever provisions we have tonight, we better take advantage of them," Charlee said as the cab driver waved them over. Everyone piled into the cabs and tried to get as comfortable as possible.

"I'm sure everyone is itching to get into the field," Charlee said to the group as she turned to look at them.

"Well, the Russian government calling in outside consultants is amazing," Jim offered from the back row of the van. "I want to be able to document as much as we can before we're forced to leave."

"I agree." Charlee nodded.

She then turned to Alf, who expanded on Jim's comment. "The Russian government usually prefer to use their own scientists. Where we're going, we'll be the first non-Russian team to research and assist with their tiger conservation. A few professors from China will be joining us. We've already spoken and are ready to collaborate on a paper once our project is done," Alton informed.

"Oh, that's great! Dr. Zhang is amazing to work with. He and I did a paper a few years ago. You'll like working with him," Charlee assured Alton with a smile.

"Will there be tension since we're American?" Alf asked, causing an uncomfortable silence to fill the air.

"It won't be because of where we're from, but there may be hostility for the simple fact that we're working to save the tigers when poaching has become a big moneymaker on the black market. Poachers will not take too kindly to us at all. The security detail that's being provided will meet us at the hotel."

"This isn't too bad," Malena noted as they climbed out of the van.

"No, not what I was expecting." The small town was picturesque and rich in history. The modern cars were out of place in a town that hadn't been renovated in over a hundred years. Charlee could easily imagine horse-drawn carriages making their way down the cobblestone streets. It was no surprise that this small town of Russia was very poor. Charlee glanced down the street and noted the small rundown buildings that had seen better years.

Their hotel was small and quaint. It wasn't the Ritz Carlton, but it sure did have a homey feel to it.

"It could be worse," Malena said, hoisting her bag over her shoulder.

"This will be perfect," Charlee smirked as they made their way into the mismatched brick building. "We won't be here long anyway. Once we've met up with everyone, into the rainforest we go."

"Hello," Malena greeted the young woman behind the counter.

"Welcome to Lyrino," the desk clerk said with heavy accented English. Charlee turned her back and rested against the counter as Malena took care of getting them checked in.

She watched as Alton, Alf, and Jim made their way into the small building with a few of their hard totes dragging behind them. Some of it would be the equipment they would need. She prayed that the rest of their things that they had shipped ahead were there at the hotel. Setting up camp was always a pain, but once everything was settled, it would be like a home away from home.

"Everything okay?" Jim asked as he came over to her side.

"Yes." She smiled. "This is definitely better than that hotel we were in when we were in India."

Jim barked out a laugh at the mention of their trip. Two years ago, they had arrived at their first destination in a small town in India, and were basically assigned huts with giant leaves for roofs. Alton and Jim quickly began updating Alf on the India trip, but Charlee didn't hear anything they were saying. Their voices faded off into the distance as her eyes were drawn to the imposing figures that stalked through the door.

Her heart just about leaped into her throat as her eyes met a set of familiar, intense eyes. She turned away quickly, trying to catch her breath.

It was him!

Weston Rogavac had officially walked into the small hotel. She turned slightly and tried to catch another peek at the entrance, but was left feeling slightly disappointed. She blew out her breath, trying to will her heart to stop racing.

"Okay, here are the keys." Malena's voice broke through Charlee's thoughts. Charlee reached out for her key, her mind still on Weston Rogavac.

"All right, time to try to get a good night's rest," Jim said to the group. "We leave bright and early. The train is set to leave at nine in the morning."

Moans and groans filled the air as the guys began to shuffle away.

"Charlee—" Malena started, but Charlee held up a hand before throwing her backpack on her back and grabbing the other from the floor.

"I'm dead on my feet, Malena," Charlee huffed, knowing that her friend probably wanted to explore the town. "I just want to try to get some uninterrupted sleep tonight."

"I was just going—"

"Goodnight." Charlee turned to walk away, but found herself facing a rock-hard chest. She was eye level with the open collar that displayed a few sprinkles of hair peeking out of the crisp white, button-up shirt. Drawing her eyes up, she was met with the same dark eyes that had plagued her dreams.

She gulped, and his eyes twinkled with laughter as he stared down at her.

"Cat got your tongue?" Malena leaned in and whispered into her ear. He must have heard her because he bursts out into laughter. She, on the other hand, prayed for the ground to open up and swallow her whole.

"Please excuse my friend. She's a little touched in the head," Charlee explained with a small smile. His friends chuckled.

"That's quite all right, Dr. Black,"Weston said.

A gasp escaped her as she realized that he knew who she was.

"Please forgive me," he rushed out, offering her his hand. "Allow me to introduce myself. My name is Weston Rogavac."

"Well, it seems as if you already know who I am," she breathed as she gripped his hand in a firm handshake.

Get a grip, girl, she thought to herself. Two seconds in his presence and she was like a cat in heat. She would need a cold shower to calm down her libido.

"It's my business to know who you are," he advised, glancing down at their still clasped hands.

"Really?" She quickly snatched her hand back, feeling her cheeks growing warm. "Why is that?"

"You have a brilliant mind. I've read all of your research. I'm a huge fan, and we have something in common," he stated, crossing his arms in front of him. Her eyes were drawn to the tan skin that was displayed, thanks to the sleeves being folded up.

"Really?" she echoed again, cringing on the inside. One would have thought that she, a doctorate prepared scientist, would have something more educated to say in response. He was filthy rich and came from old money, while she, on the other hand, was raised by blue collar parents. What on earth

could they possibly have in common? "What might that be?"

"Our love of cats."

FOUR

"What was that with you and the good doctor last night?" Luka teased.

That morning, they had boarded the train that would take them into the Far East region of Russia. He knew that Dr. Black's team was located in one of the other cars. His men sat across from him, both with curiosity brimming in their eyes.

West paused before answering, uncomfortable with their scrutiny of his initial meeting with Dr. Black. He took a sip of his water, thinking of an answer. He didn't know what had transpired between him and Dr. Black last night when they had arrived at the hotel. He could tell that she was just as flustered about meeting him as he was her. His tiger paced back and forth beneath his skin at the mere mention of Dr. Charlee Black.

"I don't know," he answered truthfully.

"If I didn't know any better, I would say that there's something between the two of you," Luka stated.

"That's not what we're here for,"West responded, staring out the window, watching the Russian scenery zoom past. Chasing after a woman was not why he traveled halfway around the world. Securing the natural habitat of the Amur tigers was his only concern. "Drago, what have you found out?" he asked, changing the subject.

"We've pinpointed where the poachers were last discovered. A few skinned animal carcasses were found about an hour north of where we'll be located." Drago reached into his attaché case and handed West a few blown-up pictures that were taken in the wild. His tiger growled at the proof of animals who had met their unfortunate ends.

Drago Pends was from a prominent tiger shifter family, extremely loyal to the Rogavac family. The Pends owned one of the top security firms in the United States, so it only made sense to put Drago in charge of security for this trip. Yes, the Russians would provide their own security, but frankly, West

didn't trust them. Drago's team was already in place at their destination, scouting out the area and securing the lands where Dr. Black's team would be working.

"Any idea who these men are?" West had to rein back on his tiger who wanted to burst forth. It wouldn't do anyone any good if he let out his pissed off tiger.

"Nomads. No names yet, sir. Once we arrive, we'll be able to track them down. We discovered a pattern of sites they've killed at. It shouldn't take long before we can track them."

"And kill them," West growled, his eyes narrowed on the pictures. His tiger pawed at his abdomen, demanding to be let out so he could go exact his revenge on the poachers.

A rumble of answering growls filled the air of the car as West handed the photos back to Drago.

"We'll take care of this," Luka stated. "We'll ensure that Dr. Black's team is not interrupted."

"I need to speak with her," West announced abruptly, standing from his seat. He didn't wait for an answer as he opened the door to their private car and stepped out into the aisle. He shut the door and took a deep breath. He walked down the hallway and found a stewardess preparing drinks and snacks for the passengers.

"Excuse me, miss," West said, gaining her attention. She jumped slightly before turning around with a large smile.

"Yes, Mr. Rogavac?" The name badge on her uniform read Darla.

"Darla, can you tell me which car Dr. Black's team is located in?" he asked.

"Of course," she answered in her thick Russian accent. "The research team is located in the car directly behind this one." She pointed down the short hallway to the door that led to the next car.

"Thank you." He nodded and headed toward the door. His heart raced with just the thought of seeing Charlee again. His tiger quieted quickly with the realization.

The sounds of the train whistle filled the air as he opened the door to the next passenger car. The lights flickered as he opened the door and stepped inside. The hairs on the back of his neck rose as the sounds of shouting echoed above.

The train was specially protected by the government, and guards were posted throughout the train, as well as on top. His attention was drawn to the sounds of a door opening. One of the men that was with Dr. Black last night stepped out with a concerned look.

"Should we be worried?" he asked West, looking up and down the empty aisle.

"I'm not sure,"West replied. He pulled his phone from his pocket and sent a quick text to Drago to check it out."I'm sure it's fine.The conductor would notify us if there was a problem."

That seemed to settle the man slightly. West's tiger huffed, unsure of the relationship between the man and Dr. Black. For some strange reason, he didn't like the thought of her in a relationship with this human male.

"I'm looking for Dr. Black," West said as he walked down the hallway. The man narrowed his eyes on West as he came to a halt in front of him.

"And what do you want with Dr. Black?" he asked cautiously.

"I'm West Rogavac."West introduced himself to the man with his hand outstretched. By the looks the man was giving him, he wouldn't just give out where she was located.West could respect that.

"I know who you are, Mr. Rogavac," he replied, giving West a firm handshake. West smirked on the inside as the human tried to size him up.West stood at least five inches taller, and had at least seventy pounds of muscle on him."I'm Dr. Jim York. I'm an acquaintance of Charlee's. She's in this car with us."

Interesting.

Dr.York had a thing for Charlee Black.

West felt a large grin spread across his face at the thought that this poor excuse of a human male had been pining after Charlee Black and she didn't even know it.

"Is everything okay out here?" a soft voice asked as the door to the private cabin opened.

West's heart began to pound as his eyes connected with Charlee's. Her dark hair was pulled into a messy bun on top of her head. She wore a short sleeve T-shirt with her university's name spread across her ample chest, and jeans that fit her like a glove. His eyes reached her feet and found perfect toes peeking out of a pair of flat leather sandals.

"Mr. Rogavac," she gasped, her eyes widening. She looked just like one of the college kids that she taught.

"Please, call me West," he said as she stepped out into the hall. His tiger stood at attention at the smile that lit up her face. Her eyes twinkled as she glanced at him.

"Well, if that's the case, you can call me Charlee. Please, come in and join us," she said, inviting him into the cabin.

West tried not to smirk as he glanced at Jim as he stepped past him.

Who was he kidding?

He threw a wink at the human male and entered the cabin behind Charlee.

"So, tell me about SPAT," Charlee asked.

West settled into his chair beside her, ignoring the angry scowl from Jim. He had to push down the cat inside of him. If he didn't know any better, he would swear his tiger wanted to purr. It was craving the feel of Charlee's hand, as if it wanted her to pet its head, or scratch behind its ears.

Down boy, he murmured to his tiger.

"I hadn't heard of your organization before this trip. Why the mystery?" she asked, her wide eyes focused on him.

"Well, it's an organization that is dear to my heart. We're not an organization that needs to be in the spotlight. We prefer to be behind the scenes so that people like yourself can be in the forefront." West glanced to the two people who sat across from him and Charlee. She had introduced Malena and Alf to him when they had entered the cabin.

"Well, that's very honorable of you," Malena noted.

"It's the right thing to do. My family has money and we have always given back. But being able to support researchers such as yourselves in preventing animals from being extinct is important to the world."

"Why tigers?" Alf asked.

West chuckled, knowing that he couldn't expand on his true interest in tigers. Humans were ignorant to the existence of shifters, and were not ready to learn of them yet. For centuries, it had been agreed that the humans would be kept in the dark on that fact.

"The tiger is considered king of all beasts. They represent power, strength, and wisdom. It's been the symbolic representation of my family for centuries," West said, fingering his family crest ring that was given to him by his father. Pride surged within his chest as he thought of one day passing this same ring down to his future son.

"Wow," Charlee breathed. "That was beautiful. The ring on your finger…is that a family crest?"

"Yes, it is." He held out his hand and his breath caught in this throat as her soft, small hand enclosed his. Her scent floated in the air, and his tiger pawed at his chest, aching to get to her.

"This is beautiful." She smiled as her eyes met his. "Look at this ring. It's almost like we're sitting amongst royalty," she joked as Malena and Alf both leaned forward to study his ring.

She wasn't too far off. In the shifter world, he was royalty.

"That's pretty cool, Mr. Rogavac," Alf said, sitting back in his chair.

"Thanks. This ring has been passed down through my family for centuries. One day, I hope to pass it down to my future son," he said, taking his hand back.

"So, is there a Mrs. Rogavac?" Malena asked with a twinkle in her eye, sending Charlee into a coughing fit.

"Yes, there is," he answered with a chuckle. "Do you need some water?" he asked Charlee, but she waved him off.

"No, I'm fine." Charlee coughed again before regaining her composure. "What does your wife think of you flying halfway around the world to help save the tigers?"

"I'm not married." He shook his head, having fun with Charlee. He could tell instantly that he liked her friend Malena. "My mother, Mrs. Rogavac, loves that her son is donating his time to help save the tigers."

FIVE

If she didn't love her best friend so much, she would kill her. Charlee stared daggers at Malena, but her friend just smiled at her, sitting there like the cat that ate the canary. Last night, after the meeting at the small hotel desk, Malena had droned on and on about Charlee needing to end her drought.

She should have never admitted to her best friend that it had been a few years since her last sexual encounter with a man. Yes, she had been on dates, but none of them had been worthy enough for Charlee to take the plunge into doing the wild mambo with any of them.

"Your mother sounds like a wonderful woman," Charlee murmured, afraid to even look him in the eyes. Her cheeks burned from embarrassment. At the mention of a wife, Charlee's throat constricted. Here she was, practically drooling over the man without even thinking he could be married.

"She is." His slight chuckle caused her to turn to him. The kindness in his eyes made her relax a little. "Tell me, Dr. Black—"

"Please, call me Charlee," she interrupted.

"Charlee. Since you seem to have a passion for the Amur tigers, what is your favorite thing about them?" he asked, leaning closer to her, his intense eyes locked on hers.

Her mind raced. This was her life's work. She could go on for hours and lecture about her favorite animal in the world. But the one answer that came to mind, she was sure he would understand. She glanced back at him, and something flashed in his odd colored eyes. For a brief second, she would have sworn they were the same as her beloved tiger.

"Well, that's an easy question. I love the grace and power that they display. When I was a child, my parents would take me to the local zoo where I first caught a glimpse of a live tiger. Her name was Seba. I swear, one look from her and I would have sworn she looked into my soul. I felt a connection, as if she were my spirit animal."

The conversations in the car drew quiet at her revelation. She looked around and found herself to be the center of attention.

"Wow, Charlee. Even I didn't know that," Malena responded with wide eyes.

"That's cool, Dr. Black," Alf said, his face filled with awe.

"I agree," West murmured, his intense eyes focused on her.

There it was again.

His eyes did that funny thing again where she would have sworn she was looking at the eyes of a tiger.

"Well, you asked—"

The screeching sound of the train's brakes filled the air as the car jerked. Bags and other items flew through the air, crashing to the floor. Charlee's body flew forward, but a strong arm kept her in place while the train fought to stop. She gripped the muscular arm as her back slammed into the seat as the train came to a halt. She fought to breathe, trying to catch her breath from having the wind knocked out of her.

"Is everyone all right," West called out to everyone in the car. Murmurs filled the air. Charlee had yet to let go of West's arm. She was shocked that the train had stopped the way it did.

"What's going on?" she asked, holding his arm tighter to her chest.

"I don't know," he murmured. "But if you let go of my arm, I'll go see what I can find out."

She jerked her head in a nod and let go. She tucked her hair behind her ear and watched him get up and check on Jim and Alton from their position in the car before stepping over to the door. Her heart pounded in her chest as the shouting again echoed above them.

"Are you okay?" Charlee asked Malena, who was sliding back into her chair. She and Alf had been thrown to the floor.

"Yes, just a little shaken up," Malena answered, looking around. "What the hell is going on?"

"I don't know," Charlee murmured. Her body jerked at the sound of short pops filling the air.

"Were those gun shots?" Alf gasped, moving toward the car window.

"Get away from the window!" West snapped. He grabbed Alf and threw him to the floor, just as a bullet pierced the window. Screams filled the air as the glass shattered. "On the floor!"

Charlee let loose a scream as more gunfire filled the air around the stopped train. She sat frozen, unable to believe that this type of violence was

occurring on what should be a peaceful trip. Her body was pulled away from the window against a hard body and thrown to the floor.

West.

She sent up a quick prayer that this was just be a nightmare, that she would wake up and find that she had dozed off on the train. But the curses and yelling let her know that this was most certainly not a dream.

Not even a nightmare.

Time seemed to stand still as silence filled the air. The only thing that Charlee could hear now was the sound of her heart pounding away. Her breaths came fast and hard as she laid there. She tried to shift her body, but the solid wall of muscle protecting her prevented movement. She jumped slightly at the sound of cell phone ringing.

"Yeah," West said into his phone, shifting his body. His warm breath blew across the back of her neck.

She rolled her eyes as her breasts pebbled from the feel of his muscular body pressed against hers. This was not the time for her body to decide to wake up, just because a sexy as sin man with the body of a God was lying on top of her.

People were shooting for Christ's sake!

Calm down, girl, she begged her traitorous body.

"Everyone okay?" he called out. Murmurs filled the air as everyone answered. "Charlee?"

"I'm good," she said as he shifted off her. She instantly missed his warmth, and his hardness pressed up against her. Maybe Malena was on to something. She could have lost her life just minutes before and here she was, turned on by the man who just literally covered her body with his to protect her.

Yup! Unfortunately, her friend was right. She needed to get laid.

West's tiger paced beneath his skin, demanding to be set free. The attack on the train was planned, and this news didn't sit well with him or his tiger. According to Drago, the attackers were trying to get to the Americans. The words weren't said aloud, but his gut told him that those men were after Charlee and her team.

"Poachers," West said as he stood with Drago outside of the train, watching the passengers exit the cars. The security team on the train had fought back and defended the train well. The attackers were driven off, and there were no reports of any injuries. "This group was bold. We're going to have to beef up our efforts to make sure that Dr. Black and her team are able to complete their assignment."

"Agreed." Drago nodded, looking around. "Preserving the tigers would cost the fuckers a lot of money."

"It was a good thing you went to their car. There's no telling what would have happened," Luka noted, crossing his arms against his chest.

"Tell me about it," West muttered, thinking of how he had to grab Charlee's student from the window.

The kid easily could have taken a bullet to the chest. His eyes casually perused the landing deck of the train, then landed on Charlee as she exited. Memories of her soft curvy body underneath him, and the faint smell of her arousal caused his tiger to just about go crazy.

Her and the members of her team had been shaken up. The stewardess and security had come and ensured that everyone was okay before moving them to a car that had not received any damages from the attack. The rest of the train ride to their final destination was in an uncomfortable silence.

He watched as her and her team moved inside of the train station.

"I take it by the way you're staring after the good doctor that we'll be keeping a close eye on her?" Luka nodded in Charlee's direction.

"Yes, we are," he murmured, picking up his bag from the ground. His feet began moving in the

direction of the entrance Charlee had disappeared into.

He could feel Drago and Luka follow behind him as they stalked into the building and through the terminal. He caught a glimpse of Charlee as she disappeared through the front door. They quickly exited the building and found Charlee talking with a gentleman by the curb. He came to an abrupt halt as he saw the two dark sedans that waited for them. The student and other professor loaded their bags into the trunks of the cars. Good. The Russian government had sent transportation for them. At least she would not be relying on public transportation to get them to their destination.

"Are we going to follow them?" Drago asked from his left.

"No, I believe we'll be at the same meeting with the Russian officials tomorrow at the sanctuary," West said as he watched them all disappear into the waiting vehicles. He didn't turn back to his men until the cars were safely on the road. His tiger wanted to know that she was secured inside her vehicle. Another black sedan pulled up along the curb of the street.

"That's us," Drago said, motioning for them to follow him to the car. West's eyes were drawn down the road to the two sedans that were barely noticeable.

His tiger huffed at the thought that Charlee was no longer near them.

Soon, he murmured to his tiger in an attempt to calm him down. We'll see her again, very soon.

SIX

"It's gorgeous, isn't it?" Charlee murmured to Malena as they both stood starstruck by the beauty of the lush surroundings.

"Yes, it is," Malena whispered.

Together they stood on the open balcony of the building that was the entranceway to the sanctuary. From where they stood, leaning against the stone banisters, they could see for miles the beautiful landscape. It was the perfect backdrop, showcasing the undisturbed nature.

Today, before leaving to go into the tiger's natural habitat, they would convene with the

Russian officials and the teams that were brought in for this study. The meeting would be starting in a few minutes.

Charlee sighed, not wanting to leave her spot on the balcony.

"Let's go," Charlee said, tapping her friend on the shoulder.

"Do we really have to?" Malena whined. "I could stay here all day and watch nature."

"It's a magnificent sight, isn't it, Dr. Black?" a heavily Russian accented voice greeted them as they walked back to the boardroom.

Charlee was certainly impressed. How could anyone get any meetings done with a view like that? The large boardroom, with one complete wall made of impeccable glass windows displaying the beautiful scenery, housed a magnificent oak table in the center with sturdy leather chairs surrounding it. On each end of the room, large plasma televisions were mounted on the walls.

"It is, Mr. Yakovich." Charlee smiled as she stopped in front of Tryndin Yakovich, the Russian government official that would be leading the meeting this morning.

He was dressed in a perfectly tailored dark suit. He was a nice looking older man, who appeared to take good care of himself. The sly smile that graced his lips, and the way his eyes seemed to devour

Charlee, made her stomach queasy. But she didn't let it sway her from being professional. She was used to working with men during her career, which was a mostly male-driven profession. She stood up taller and didn't shy away from him. She could deal with him like she had all the other chauvinistic males before him.

"I'm sure it will be even more beautiful in person," Malena said with a nod of her head.

"Oh, it is." He nodded. "Everyone on this mission should be considered lucky. Humans are normally not allowed out in the sanctuary. We try to keep it as natural as can be so that the tigers and other wild animals can live in the most natural habitat that we could create."

"What you all have done here is amazing," Charlee said. "And by the looks of it, not cheap either. It must have taken years, and lots of money to accomplish something like this."

"We've been lucky that our government understands the importance of maintaining the eco system and preserving the Amur tigers. We want to do everything we can to ensure that they do not go extinct."

People began to file into the boardroom as he continued to speak. Charlee's eyes began to wander around the room, taking in the rest of her team, as

well as Dr. Zhang and his team, and a few others that she was unfamiliar with.

"I believe we better have a seat. It looks like everyone is here," Charlee said as she excused herself, pulling Malena behind her.

"He was going to talk our ears off," Malena murmured as they slid into their chairs where they had left their belongings.

"I figured." Charlee nodded, then smiled at Alton and Jim as they settled into their chairs. Alf had been assigned to go ahead with the rest of the team and assist with getting their camp set up.

Another gentleman walked up to Tryndin and whispered something in his ear. Curiosity got the best of Charlee, and she strained to hear what they were talking about. But, unfortunately, she didn't speak Russian and was clueless on what they were whispering about so passionately.

Worry began to fill her chest. After the events on the train, she was left feeling a little uneasy. She had never been involved in a shoot-out before, much less been shot at. Since the train, everything seemed to calm down. The Russian government had assured them that their security would be tightened and they would have no worries.

Once they left the train station and drove the hour to Kovodsk, everything had been smooth sailing. They were even lucky with the accommodations the previous night. They stayed in a small bed and breakfast that was not luxurious by any standards, but it was clean, and the people were very hospitable.

"Is something wrong, gentlemen?" Jim asked from his seat.

"Everything is fine." Tryndin nodded as the other gentlemen walked out of the room. "Let's get on with the meeting, shall we?" He moved to the head of the table. Charlee and Malena both opened up their notebooks in order to take notes.

"That was weird," Malena leaned over and whispered. Charlee nodded as Tryndin began.

"I'm not quite sure if you all know each other. I would like to start off with introductions, if you don't mind going around the table and introducing yourselves." Tryndin motioned to the gentleman sitting to his right as he took his seat at the head of the table.

"Good morning, everyone. Welcome to Kovodsk. My name is Dr. Lev Ilyich, and I am one of the local ecologist for the sanctuary."

Charlee murmured a greeting along with everyone else as the next man introduced himself as Dr. Velimir Igorevich, the local senior researcher. They had made it halfway through the room before the doors burst open to the conference room. Charlee jumped as the door banged against the wall.

Her heart pounded in her chest as her eyes flew to the door to see who was causing all the commotion.

Weston Rogavac.

A very pissed off Weston Rogavac.

"I know you knew that I was here, Tryndin," Weston snapped, his glowering eyes locked on the Russian official as he stalked into the room.

The two men who were with him before, trailed behind him. Charlee's eyes widened as she took in the power that he displayed. The official jumped from his seat, almost knocking the chair over. His face flushed red as he began to spew words in his native language.

If there were a time that Charlee wished she could speak Russian, it would be now.

"It was not necessary for you to be here," Tryndin insisted, speaking in Russian.

West was pissed that the Russian government tried to hide the meeting by telling them the wrong time.

"I don't need an excuse to come to the sanctuary," West snapped in his family's native tongue. His tiger paced back and forth beneath his skin. It wanted to swipe its heavy paw at the official, to wipe away the disrespectful look that crossed the man's face. How

dare the Russian official try to insinuate that he was not needed.

He didn't have to have an excuse to be there. The Rogavac family donated a hefty sum of money to ensure that the sanctuary would have everything it needed to get off and running. Therefore, he had every right to be there.

"You can't just barge in on a private meeting—"

West held up his hand to cut the Russian official off. He could feel Luka and Drago behind him, as they too were pissed at the additional information that they had learned this morning. West had received an email with information about the latest poacher's kill. A couple of men had been arrested two days ago by the local authorities, due to the discovery of a dead cat in the back of their truck. The information was kept from the public.

Another innocent tiger killed for his bones and skin.

"I can do what I want. It seems to me that poaching has been increasing since the sanctuary was opened. The purpose of the sanctuary was to provide a safe refuge for tigers." West moved to an empty chair across from Charlee. His eyes briefly met hers to find shock written across her face.

"We are working on the poacher problem," Tryndin sputtered as Luka and Drago placed themselves around the room.

"Well, work harder," West demanded, sending a hard glare in the official's direction. "My men and I are here to stay, and we're going on this expedition. It's time that I personally inspect this sanctuary that my family helped pay for."

Tryndin paused, his mouth pressed into a hard line, as if holding back further words. West eyed the man, daring him to say more. He knew he had the official literally by the balls.

If his family ceased the monetary donations that they gave every year, the sanctuary would suffer. Tryndin, a human, didn't understand the real reason the Rogavac's donated so much money. Not that they would actually let the tigers suffer, but if it was on the table that they would pull from being a heavy contributor to one of Russia's beloved gems, that would certainly come under scrutiny in the public, therefore castrating Mr. Tryndin Yakovich.

"Very well," Tryndin conceded as he switched back to English. "Please excuse us for the interruption. We are lucky to have Mr. Weston Rogavac joining us. Let's move on with the meeting, shall we?"

West nodded to everyone around the room. His eyes again found their way to Charlee's wide ones. He softened slightly as he gazed into her hazel eyes. She sent a small smile his way before turning back to Tryndin as he began his presentation.

Tryndin went on to speak on the history of the sanctuary and all that it offered. West, familiar with the history, took the time to study the room, watching as they took notes and asked questions. Each researcher and scientist were brilliant and at the peak of their careers. West's eyes made their way back to Charlee and discreetly took her in.

His tiger pushed against his chest. He wanted the sexy wildlife biologist. Everything about her was downright sexy, and he ached to have her. From her thick, dark hair that hung in waves around her shoulders, covering her creamy tan skin, dropping down to her full breasts and thick hips that he knew called for him.

His tiger wanted to nuzzle her neck and breathe in her scent again. It was a scent that was addictive. In the train, his cat literally purred as it surrounded him.

"How many cats have been tagged?" Charlee's voice broke through West's thoughts.

"About five or so. As I'm sure you all know, it is difficult to catch a glimpse of a tiger in it's natural habitat. One of the goals for this mission would be to tag a few more," Dr. Nardin Skobo, the Russian wildlife biologist, disclosed to the room.

"I'm glad you brought up the mention of tagging," Luka interrupted, standing from his chair.

He walked over to the computer that controlled the massive television displays.

West nodded his head to his longtime friend, knowing that Luka would inform the room of the latest technology that they had brought with them. Luka, a biomedical engineer, was a genius. He had developed a microchip that would change the way that any animal could be tracked.

"At Rogavac Industries, our focus is always advancing technologies that will be efficient. We have come up with a microchip that has just been approved for active use in tracking animals in the wild." Luka brought up his presentation on the screens for the room to view. He began describing how the microchip would not only work as a GPS to track where the tigers were, but could also share information about the tiger, such as vital signs, and if the tiger was ill or injured, it would send an alert to the scientists so that they could track it down to assess it in person.

"Wow," Charlee breathed out, just as Luka finished his impromptu presentation. "That certainly would make the life of a wildlife biologist easier. According to your information, if a tiger dies in the wild, we would be notified almost in real time, and that would allow us to obtain the body and study it."

"Exactly," Luka said with a nod. Excitement filled the room as murmurs and chatter increased.

"I think this is great," Dr. Zhang commented. "This will also help us with our research. One of the latest projects we are working on is trying to understand why some of the Amurs are migrating from Russia to China."

"Exactly." Dr. York nodded in agreement. "This will help us determine if something is wrong in the ecosystem."

"Well, gentlemen, I think we have all the information we need," Charlee announced to the room as she stood. "I don't know about you, but I'm ready to get into the wild."

SEVEN

Charlee bustled around the massive tent, gathering supplies that she would need. The base camp had been set up and it was amazing. It was like a mini city crammed into a corner of the national park. They didn't want to spread out too far into the wild since human contact with the natural habitat was rare. They had Land Rovers for their longer trips, and even some of them planned to walk to try to keep as much of the reservation undisturbed.

Alf and the other members of her team had set up their tent and did an amazing job. She was truly impressed with her graduate student. He would make an amazing scientist. She glanced around at the enormous tent that housed their portable laboratory. The tent was bustling with people as they prepared for the expedition.

"The tranqs are in the cooler," Malena noted as she continued to type on the computer.

"Perfect." Charlee nodded as she moved toward the small fridge that sat on one of the counters. She opened it to count how many they had. Ten. Perfect. Hopefully, they would come across that many tigers, but she doubted it.

"Dr. Black, I've already loaded the tranq guns into the vehicles," Alf announced as he entered the tent. "The portable generators are all charged and loaded into the trucks."

"Thanks, Alf." She sent a smile his way before he moved to the side to speak to one of Jim's assistants.

"The accommodations that the sanctuary provided us with have been amazing," Malena said.

"I know," Charlee agreed as she continued to gather items that they would need to take with them.

They were both used to sleeping in the tiny tents that barely covered their bodies. But these were big enough to stand and move around in, and room enough for two women to sleep. The men would all bunk together in their own tents.

She continued to mark things off her checklist as she found them around the tent. They wouldn't

be able to take computers, so she grabbed the tablets that would send data back to the main portable lab where Alton and the other senior researchers would be working.

They would all break up into teams. Charlee and the other species specialist and assistants would be the ones going into the wild to track down and tag the tigers. Jim and the other ecologist would be going on their own expeditions to explore and study the soil, plant life, and water supply, while the senior researchers would stay in camp, analyzing and processing all the data that would be transmitted back to them.

"Where are the night vision goggles?" Charlee asked, looking up from her checklist. They would definitely need those. They would be tracking at all times of day, but night was usually the best time to find a tiger in motion.

"Down on that bottom shelf." Alf pointed from where he stood.

Charlee moved over to the shelf and knelt down. The cases that held the goggles had tipped back all the way, and her short arms were unable to reach them.

"Thanks," Charlee muttered as she reached for them.

"Charlee!" Malena called out.

"Hold your horses," Charlee called back, crawling farther onto the bottom row. She would hate to have to move the whole shelving unit just to reach them. Her feet flailed in the air, just as her fingers grabbed the strap to the case that held the goggles. "Got it!" she exclaimed, wiggling her bottom in celebration.

She crawled backward with her prize and onto her knees, only to discover a pair of sturdy boots standing next to her. She paused before her eyes traveled up the very muscular body attached to the boots, and was met with the very amused eyes of Weston Rogavac.

After ensuring that all details of their business were solidified, West decided to go look for Charlee. Drago and his team had already disappeared into the wild. West was sure that his security specialists had already shifted to blend in. They would be discrete, and they knew to avoid the areas that the humans would be exploring. West would hate for the humans to accidentally tranq and tag a shifter instead of a natural tiger. It would be very hard to explain how a tiger flew back to the United States.

Luka had disappeared with the Chinese scientist to talk future projects, leaving West on his own for the moment. He was sure that Charlee would be busy gearing up to begin tracking, but he had to see her.

The sight that met his eyes when he entered her portable tent took his breath away. Her friend, with a wide grin on her face, had pointed to where her world-renowned professor was. His eyes landed on her plump ass dancing in the air as she crawled backward from beneath a storage unit.

Pure lust slammed into his chest at the sight of her perfect rear end. His hands itched to grab her hips so that he could thrust his cock deep inside her from behind. He blinked and shook his head, quickly changing his wayward thoughts. His tiger loved where his mind was going, and so did his cock.

"What do you have there?" he joked, holding out a hand to help her stand.

Fascination gripped him as he watched a pink hue spread across her cheeks. He had to shut off the part of his brain that got a rush from the sight of her on her knees in front of him. He didn't want to scare the sexy doctor away with a massive erection in her face in front of all her colleagues.

"Night vision goggles," she chuckled, taking his outstretched hand. His larger hand engulfed hers as she stood.

"Ah, so you can see in the dark." He nodded, instantly disappointed when she let his hand go. He

followed behind her as she moved toward a table where a large backpack sat.

"So what brings you here?" she asked, curiosity shining in her eyes.

You, he wanted to say, but bit his tongue.

"I wanted to check on you and your team to ensure that you had everything you would need." He looked around the tent and held in a chuckle. Everyone was acting as if they were so busy, but he could easily tell they were all trying not to get caught eavesdropping.

"Yes, we're good," she responded with a wide grin, excitement plastered across her face. His heart skipped a beat with how much she loved tigers. He had to push his tiger back. West knew that he would have to shift tonight to let his tiger out. Leaving a tiger contained for too long made the beast agitated, and right now, his animal was demanding it.

To get to Charlee.

It wanted her.

And so did the man.

"Will you be going out with one of the teams?" she asked, leaning against the table. His eyes followed her hand as she tucked her hair behind her ear, and traveled to her mouth. He swallowed hard as he stared at her plump lips. Licking his own, he imagined brushing them against hers, just to get a taste. He was sure they would be as sweet as berries.

"Yes." He coughed, trying to steer his thoughts away from anything sexual, but was finding that hard to do. She evoked this response from him, and his animal loved it.

Need flashed in her eyes and his tiger knew that they would be the one to fulfill that need. She bit her lip, and he had to hold back the instinct to grab her and toss her over his shoulder, to carry her to his private tent where he could spend hours exploring every facet of her body.

Not now, he promised his animal, but soon.

"Yes, I can be of assistance."

"Really? How so?" she asked playfully with a tilt of her head.

He smiled. The good doctor would get to know him soon enough. The tiger in him wanted to come forward to show her just how he could help.

"I'm a master tracker. I'll be able to assist in finding as many tigers as you want."

"Wow, really?" she breathed as her eyes grew wide. "I would love to hear someday how you learned to track."

She was openly flirting with him now, and he was captivated by her flirtatious smile. Two could play that game.

He leaned in close to her and lowered his voice. "Anytime you're ready, I'd be willing to take you out so I can show you my many skills."

EIGHT

"He wants you," Malena announced as she climbed into her cot and fluffed her pillow.

Charlee ignored her friend as she set the alarm clock. She shook her head, thinking of how early they were going to have to get up in the morning.

Early bird gets the worm.

Their first destination, where they would attempt to find a tiger, was over three hundred miles away. Weston seemed to be confident that he would be able to track the tigers down.

Weston.

Just the thought of him brought a warm and cuddly feeling into her chest and an ache to her core. She climbed into the sleeping bag that was placed on her cot.

"He's so out of my league," Charlee sighed, staring up at the ceiling of the tent.

"So what? He's loaded," Malena said, shutting off the lamp and casting them into darkness. "That's a bonus. But his eyes don't lie. He wanted to swallow you up whole."

Charlee giggled. That's why she loved her best friend so. Being able to travel around the world as part of her career with Malena was a bonus. Nights spent in tents like this reminded Charlee of their undergraduate days in the dorm rooms.

"You're seeing things," Charlee insisted. Her attempt at flirting with Weston totally backfired on her. She couldn't help herself. Here she was, an accomplished professor with multiple renowned publications in the top journals, and one look from Weston made her realize that she was still a woman.

A woman who wanted a man who was out of her league.

"I'll bet you he has a thing for sexy nerds," Malena joked.

"Nerd?" Charlee scoffed.

"Yes, you're a nerd. I hate to break it to you, but yes, you are definitely nerd material. A sexy one at that."

"I'll take it and own it," Charlee laughed. Malena's giggle floated across the room. She missed their pretend slumber parties. Charlee sat up and stared off in the direction of Malena. "You really think I have a chance?"

"You are far more better looking than those models and celebrities that he's seen with in public. And you have a gorgeous brain to go along with it. He'll be able to have an actual conversation with you, unlike those bimbos."

"Thanks, Malena," Charlee groaned, throwing her arm over her face as her friend continued her pep talk.

"But seriously, Charlee, if you like him, go after him." Malena yawned, and Charlee could hear the rustle of blankets from the other side of the room. "I want you to be happy, and if that means you having an amazing fling on the other side of the world, then so be it. What have you got to lose?"

Charlee became lost in her own thoughts as Malena became silent. Malena was right. What did she have to lose? She had a great career, savings, and a nice place to live. Why couldn't she just toss caution to the wind and have a steamy love affair with a sexy man who just so happened to love tigers as much as she did?

She rolled over onto her side as she began to drift off, with the images of Weston in the forefront of her mind. She pulled the covers over her shoulders and snuggled beneath the sleeping blanket, remembering his smile and the scent of him as he had leaned closer to her to whisper in her ear. A shiver snaked its way down her spine with the memory of his words in her ear.

For once, Charlee would let loose and let go. She would take the chance and see what happened between the two of them. Who knew what it could morph into. Lust? Love? Steamy affair? Marriage? Charlee smiled as she drifted off to sleep. She couldn't wait to see what the future held.

His cat was finally free and loved the feel of the moon in the sky and the open ground beneath his paws. West and Luka had shifted to prowl the night to begin tracking where the natural tigers would be. Drago and a few of his men were searching another area of the park so that they could cover as much terrain as they could.

In their tiger forms, they could cover more ground faster. Even in cat form, West was still in control of his animal. He had a close bond with it, and could trust his animal when it was in the forefront. The smells of the wild were a bit of a distraction for his cat, causing him to have to rein it in a few times. It wanted to go discover the new area, and chase after a small animal or two that they came across.

Thanks to Drago's research, they knew where most of the cameras where hidden on the grounds so that they could avoid them. They wouldn't want the humans to catch sight of one of them in their shifted forms, confusing them with one of the tigers in the sanctuary. There was no difference between West's tiger and a non-shifter tiger. Only shifters could tell the difference.

He glanced over to his right to find Luka trotting next to him. With the number of Amur tigers dwindling, it was unlikely that they would just run into one tonight. But West wanted to look for trails of the tigers so that in the morning, he would be able to lead Charlee and the others in the right direction.

His tiger let loose a low, drawn out growl at the mention of Charlee. His heart stuttered at just the thought of her attempt to flirt with him. He couldn't resist laying it on thick with his reply. She was the kind of intelligent, sexy professor that young boys would have wet dreams about. The only thing she was missing was a set of large framed glasses.

Add those, and she would be the epitome of a sexy nerd Goddess. Just what West loved in a woman—intelligence that dripped sex appeal. Just being around the sexy professor kept West in a state of sexual frustration.

Luka's chuff snagged West's attention, causing him to slow to a stop. Luka's tiger pawed something on the ground, underneath a thick bush. He looked up and nodded his head in the direction. West walked over to where Luka was and he too pawed and sniffed the ground.

Tiger scent.

They were on the correct path of a female tiger. The scent was a few days old. Once they had a general idea of a location of the female, then Charlee and her team could track her and tag her. West knew that it was imperative that they get the new microchips on the tigers. This would change the future and allow them to gather more in-depth data then they could with the older versions of ear tags.

Luka led the way along a path between a thick brush of trees. They traveled for an hour in complete silence before finally slowing down. West's ears perked up. The woods had become deathly silent. The hairs on the back of his neck rose and he slowed. Luka must have picked up on it too. His keen amber eyes turned to West, and West nodded his head to confirm that he noticed the shift in the forest.

A yip in the distance caught their ears. It couldn't be! West moved to the edge of the brush and peeked out. His eyes, with their perfect shifter sight, took in the female tiger coming out of her den, carved into the side of a steep hill, with a kitten in her mouth and two rolling around in the grass, pouncing on each other. Luka crept up next to West in awe. This was an amazing discovery. A tigress having birthed three cubs while living in the sanctuary was an accomplishment worth celebrating.

West and Luka glanced at each other. A lazy tiger grin spread across Luka's feline face, and West was sure one was plastered on his too, but those grins of excitement and happiness quickly went out the window at the next sound that echoed through the air.

The slight cocking sound of a weapon.

West glanced around and quickly saw the moonlight reflect off the barrel of a shotgun sticking out of the brush from the other side of the hill.

He stepped from the brush and headed toward the humans that were hidden in the trees. Rage burned within his chest that these humans would try to kill the tigress, or worse, her cubs. Luka was right behind him as they moved toward the humans, not even hiding anymore. West would rather take a bullet meant for the female. As a shifter, his genetics would allow him to heal from a bullet. The female and her cubs would not.

Voices could be heard muttering in another language. West finally caught sight of three human males. Shock was registered on their faces at the sight of two large Amur tigers stalking their way. Both West and Luka's tigers were well over fourteen feet long, topping over seven hundred pounds.

West's cat was ready to tear the humans limb to limb. No one would know out here in the wild. Who would care? The men didn't deserve to live for what they were about to do, and probably had done many times already. The lowly humans were one of the main reasons for the tiger population diminishing.

The one human brought his gun up and aimed it at West. A familiar presence at his side signaled that Luka was next to him. West didn't dare take his eyes off the humans, and he knew that Luka was ready to attack. Continuous growls resonated from Luka as he too waited to see what the humans would do.

West flashed his massive fangs and let loose a roar as he planted his paws wide and stood his ground in the line of fire. If the human attempted to fire at the female tiger, he would certainly hit West first.

A hiss from the far left announced the presence of another tiger, that appeared to be coming from around the edge of the hill. Two more tigers followed behind it.

Drago and his men.

Curses could be heard from the humans as the tigers made a stand against them. West released a hiss, again showing his fangs and displaying his alpha status. He was practically daring the humans to shoot. They would get off one or two good shots before being mauled to death by five pissed off tigers.

The shifters made their intentions very clear. They would protect the tigress and her cubs to the death. The humans would not have enough bullets to stop all five tigers.

Reality must have hit home for the humans as the sounds of them scurrying off into the woods filled the air. West released a loud roar that echoed off into the night. His cat begged to give chase, but he held it at bay. One swipe from his tiger's massive paw would crush them. It was tempting, but West was satisfied that they got the point. Next time, he wouldn't be so lenient.

The tigress and cubs were safe for now. He turned his head and found her at the mouth of her den, cubs nowhere to be found. She must have pushed them into the den when she picked up on the danger. Her curious eyes looked around at the five tigers that had protected her and her cubs. West knew that this was a sight to behold, and rare. It was

not often that tigers came together. They were shy in nature, and preferred a life of solitude.

It was time to leave. They would need to be back at the campground before the humans realized they were missing. At first light, they would bring the humans here to tag the tigress and her cubs.

NINE

The steady sway of the vehicle on any other day would have lulled Charlee to sleep. But today was not just any day. Today, she was deep in Panthera National Park on the search for wild tigers. Just the thought of getting up close and personal with the tigers was enough to send her heart racing.

Right now, though, her heart had another reason to almost jump from her chest. Weston was driving the off-road Land Rover that had been outfitted for such an excursion. She still didn't know what the argument between him and Mr. Yakovich was about. She assumed it had something to do with the sanctuary, but whatever it had been, it was apparent that Weston had won.

Even though her alarm went off way earlier than she would have liked, just knowing that she would be on a month-long journey in the wild with Weston had her dragging a grumbling Malena out of bed so that they would be on time. It wasn't like she could get dressed up with makeup and heels out in the wild, so the only thing she could do to feel the least bit sexy was leave her hair down. Usually, her thick mess stayed in a bun for a whole trip, but the look in his eyes when they landed on her when they arrived at the trucks let her know she had made the right decision.

Malena was having a light conversation with Dr. Skobo, from the Russian team, in the back seat. Their truck led the way, with the other Land Rover carrying members of another team behind them as Weston expertly navigated the rugged road.

She glanced out the window, loving the view. The plush green lands were achingly beautiful. She rolled the window down and picked up her camera to catch a quick snapshot. She wanted to make sure that she had pictures to document every aspect of their trip. The view of the sun rising over the grassy plains was downright breathtaking. She was able to get some amazing shots, and she couldn't wait until she got home so that she could get the photos developed.

"It shouldn't be too much longer before we reach our destination." Weston's voice broke through her thoughts. "If you want to sometime, I can show you where you can get some amazing shots."

"Really?" she asked, turning to him. He nodded his head as he kept his eyes on the narrow dirt road. "I thought the sanctuary didn't allow humans in it?"

"Well, when your family has donated millions to help fund such a place, you tend to get special treatment." He chuckled as he glanced at her.

"Oh!" she gasped, her mind focusing on his mention of his families donated millions.

"I'm kidding," he said at her reaction. "The closest we were allowed was by a helicopter flying above. I've flown a chopper over this national park many times, and have practically memorized every beautiful peak and valley of this place."

She barked out a nervous laugh at the thoughts of being out of her league with him. She shook her head and pushed the thoughts away. She may not know how to get an affair started, but she was a fast learner.

"So tell me about yourself," she asked him, wanting to make idle conversation. They had been in the truck for a couple of hours, and by the looks of the GPS, they should be arriving at their destination in less than an hour.

"What do you want to know?" he asked, his lips tilted up in a devious smile.

"Who's running your business while you're here?" She turned to him in her seat to secretly watch him. As if sensing her attention, he threw her a smile.

"Well, there are a lot of people who work under me who are great at their jobs, and make mine even easier. I have a fantastic secretary who is holding down the fort and making sure that everyone is staying on task. What about you? Who's teaching the world-renowned Dr. Charlee Black's classes while she's traipsing across the world?"

"Well, I too have a kick ass secretary who has arranged coverage for all of my classes, and will run my office until I return."

"Ellen is amazing," Malena chimed in from the back seat. "Charlee wouldn't know how to put on her shoes without that woman."

"Good. Trusting people are hard to find," West murmured with a nod. "What else do you want to know?" He turned his keen eyes toward her.

She had a list of questions, but figured being packed in a car with two other people listening to their conversation was not the best time to really get to know him. So she decided to keep it easy.

"I see you speak Russian. What other languages do you speak?" She smiled, glancing back and catching Malena's eye, who in turn threw her a wink. Charlee rolled her eyes before turning back to Weston.

"My parents were from Russia. I was born there, but was primarily raised in the States. But I'm also fluent in Spanish, Arabic, and Italian."

"It's good to know that you're fluent in many languages, Mr. Rogavac. But I still don't understand why you're on this trip? Everyone here are scientists, trying to ensure the survival of the Amur tigers. What do you get out of this trip?" Dr. Skobo asked from the back seat.

The vehicle jerked to a sudden halt. Charlee would have sworn the temperature in the truck dropped a few degrees by the cold, hard glare that Weston sent the Russian scientist. Her breath caught in her throat at the balls of Dr. Skobo. She turned and met the shocked eyes of Malena.

What the hell was that?

"We're here," Weston announced dryly, jerking the gearshift into park.

Charlee glanced around and found them to be literally in the middle of nowhere.

Let the tracking begin.

The group moved through the woods, following West and Luka as they led the way. Before leaving the trucks, West and Luka made sure that all of them had some sort of weapon on them. Even though they were in a national park, it was still considered the wild. He and Luka would be able to pick up on a threat due to their tigers, but he didn't want to take a chance. Just in case the humans got separated, he wanted to make sure that they were prepared.

West knew that they had to put on a front, as if they had never been there before. It would draw too many questions about how they knew where the tigress was.

West cursed himself when he realized that he had made a mistake in the truck when he offered to take Charlee to a few spots to capture photographs. He couldn't help the slip. He was captivated by the emotions that graced her face as she took her pictures. The wind blowing in the open window, moving her hair away from her face, displayed her features perfectly. It had him wishing that he had a camera to capture all her different expressions.

He hadn't actually lied about flying over the national park multiples time. He had. He truly came to know the park over the years by sneaking into it with Luka as their tigers. Not even the Russian

officials knew, who were so set on keeping him from the park.

The scientist questioning him about why he was there solidified his suspicions. Something was going on that they didn't want the top investors to know about. But what?

He stopped to bend down, pretending to study a track. It was the tigress' paw print, but he had to play the part.

"We're headed in the right direction," he said as he stood.

"Wow, you're good," Charlee murmured, looking around the dense trees.

"West is the best," Luka chuckled, slapping him on the back. "He could find a needle in a haystack."

"I'm not that good," he objected with a shake of his head. It was the tiger in him. Tigers weren't known for their sense of smell. His tiger just had a great sense of direction.

"Still, it's impressive. We're making great time." She came to stand beside him as Luka moved on with the others, brushing past them to follow him, leaving them alone. "It certainly would have taken us much longer to find the trail."

A gentle smile graced his lips as he took her in. She had finally pulled her hair into a messy bun on top of her head. His fingers ached to pull it out so that he could watch it tumble around her shoulders.

He ached to see what her hair would look like spread across his pillows back home.

With it being summer, the dense woods were muggy, and everyone was sporting sweat spots on their clothes. She was no different, but she made it work for her. Sweat lined her face, and the heat made her look flushed. His eyes followed her hand as she took out a small hand towel from her pocket. He stepped closer to her, watching her eyes widen as he took the towel from her hand.

He gently reached up and wiped the sweat from her forehead, trailing the towel down her temples and around to her nose to wipe the little drops of moisture that accumulated there. He couldn't resist leaning in and covering her mouth with his.

His tiger went wild with the first taste of her. His hand cupped her face gently as he angled his head and deepened the kiss. Her tongue didn't shy away from his as it invited him in farther. A moan escaped her as she leaned in hard against him, crushing her ample breasts to his chest. The kiss turned urgent, and a voice in the back of his mind signaled for him to stop. In the middle of the forest with their group not too far away was not how he wanted to have her.

"We better stop," he murmured against her lips before pulling away. The scent of her arousal drove his tiger wild. Her eyes opened, and the lust that he saw there made his cock ache even more. "Don't look at me like that, or you'll find yourself with your back against a tree and my cock buried deep in your pussy. Fast."

She gasped at his words and closed her eyes as he leaned his forehead against hers, breathing in her scent. His cat demanded that they take her, but he had to push his animal back down.

"That doesn't sound too bad, Weston," she breathed, a smile spreading across her face as her eyes opened.

"Don't test me, Charlee. And it's West. I think we're past the formal names." He grinned, grabbing her hand. "Let's catch up with the group before Luka sends back a search party."

They quickly walked through the brush, catching up with the others. Their hands remained joined, but he refused to let her go. Her smaller hand belonged in his much larger one. He didn't care what it looked like when they reached the group. She tried to pull her hand away from his, but he tightened his grip on her. His cat didn't want to let her out of its sight, much less its reach.

The path narrowed, and they all had to walk in a single file line. He directed Charlee to walk ahead of him so that he could pull up the rear. Luka knew the way, but for safety reasons, he wanted to keep his eye on Charlee.

He still couldn't shake off the uneasy feeling from the train. In speaking with Tryndin, he refused the Russian security, not trusting them. His men would do fine and keep everyone safe. Drago was the master of stealth. West knew that he and his men were around them, but they wouldn't present themselves unless they needed to.

Luka held up a hand, signaling to the group to stop. He turned and his eyes met West's. They had arrived.

"He's found it," West murmured, stepping close to Charlee.

Her eyes flickered to his, and he could see the excitement bubbling inside of her. This was her career, what she lived for. His tiger was pleased that she loved cats as much as she did. Her passion for them was evident in every aspect of her career. West had read all of her journal articles and publications.

They would have to be as silent as they could be. They didn't want the tigress to pick up on the group. If she did, it would go one of two ways; either she would grab her cubs and run, or she would stand her ground and defend her den.

West knew that they were still far enough to keep a safe distance away from the tigress that she shouldn't be able to pick up on their scent or hear them. By the looks of the cubs the night before, they were still young enough that the tigress wouldn't

leave the den much. He knew that it wouldn't be until they were about six months old before they would start their adventures away from the den so that she could teach them how to hunt.

"Let's tag you a tiger," he whispered.

TEN

The natural sounds of the wild surrounded them. Charlee's heart still pounded in her chest from the kiss. And oh boy, what a kiss it was. She had been two seconds away from ripping Weston's clothes from his body when he pulled back. Deep down, she was pleased that he had been effected by the kiss as much as she was. That was the type of kiss that poets wrote about. She had certainly seen stars the minute his lips brushed hers.

West had yet to leave her side as they moved into position. Excitement bubbled in her chest at seeing the first tiger in its natural habitat. She knelt down with her high-powered binoculars as Weston moved the brush aside. She glanced around with the binoculars and froze in place.

Tiger.

And she wasn't alone. There were three tiger cubs too!

"You're going to catch something flying by if you don't close your mouth," West murmured, prompting her to snap her mouth closed.

"Do you see this! This is amazing. This is—" Her thoughts were running a mile a minute. This was historical. The purpose of the sanctuary was to save endangered species, and because of this place, a tigress was able to produce and raise not one cub, but three.

She glanced around and saw everyone had the same look of excitement and awe on their faces as they watched the tigress lay on the lush green grass as the cubs played on and around her. She promptly ignored the cubs as they jumped and pounced on each other. Everyone began documenting, photographing, and videoing the feline family. Each member of the team had been designated with a job back at the main camp before the trip.

She found Alf posted with one of his video cameras, documenting the family. She couldn't wait to see what he would capture. Malena and Dr.

Zhang's assistant worked to prepare the tranquilizer guns.

She lost track of time as she frantically snapped shots of the cats. A sensation came over her, as if she were being watched. She glanced over at West and found his eyes on her. She smiled softly, feeling her cheeks warm at his attention. Her core pulsated with the thoughts of the two of them naked, sweaty, in a tangled mess on a large bed. His eyes dropped to her lips, and she couldn't help but to nibble on her lower lip with her teeth. His eyes darkened with her action.

She quickly turned away and snapped the last few shots she could while trying to catch her breath. She couldn't believe how much he affected her with just a look.

But now, it was time to break up this lazy afternoon nap for the momma tiger.

"Dr. Zhang and Dr. Skobo, we should go ahead and tranq the momma," Charlee said, standing from her spot to walk over to the other biologists.

"I don't think we need to tranq the cubs," Dr. Zhang offered, his words heavily accented.

"I agree. " Dr. Skobo nodded, standing with his hands on his hips. "The cubs look like they're young enough to where we can just grab them and insert the chip."

"Yes, and we need to make sure that momma is totally out first." Charlee motioned for Malena to bring her one of the tranq rifles.

"I hear this is your first trip in almost a year. Sure your aim isn't rusty?" Zhang joked.

"Never that." Charlee laughed, checking the rifle out. "My aim is still true."

Growing up, her father had taken her and her siblings hunting quite often. Arthur Black believed that women should know how to shoot a gun just as well as a man. As children, her, her sister Ruby, and brother Dane, never missed a hunting trip with their father. It was a great bonding experience between a father and his children. Even to this day, they all gathered once a year for a hunt.

"You sure you know how to work that?" Luka joked.

"Somebody distract the momma and I'll show you all how to tranq a tiger."

West and Luka volunteered to distract the momma tiger. Charlee had found a perfect position that would allow her to easily hit her target. She'd had to move a little closer to guarantee a hit. She was good, but at over three hundred feet, she wanted to make sure she hit what she was aiming for. They didn't have too many tranqs, and she couldn't afford to waste even one.

"Come on, Momma," she murmured as she peered through the scope. The barrel of the lightweight rifle fit comfortably in her arms. She locked on her target and waited for the tigress to awaken from her nap.

Alf and Malena were silent as they stood behind her, while West and Luka had disappeared to create their distraction. Charlee was patient as she waited. "A patient hunter is a successful hunter," her father had always said. Charlee waited for the right opportunity to appear.

The tigress' ears flickered and her tail curled slightly. Charlee strained to hear what the tiger may have heard.

There it was again. A chuffing sound.

Charlee knew that chuffing was the way that tigers communicated. It was a friendly noise that caught the tigress' attention. Her large head came up from the grass as she looked around.

Charlee waited still.

Not yet.

The tiger looked around, apparently not seeing anything.

The chuffing sound could be heard again. Was another tiger in the area? Charlee flexed her finger on the trigger. If there was another tiger in the area, she had another tranquilizer loaded and could easily tranq another one.

Finally, the momma tiger moved to stand and stretched as she did, dislocating one of the cubs who were trying to hold onto her. The tigress was a beauty. She had to be about twelve feet long. She was magnificent as she stood above her cubs, looking in the direction of the chuffing.

Now.

Charlee pulled the trigger.

Bullseye.

The tigress let loose a growl as she swung around in Charlee's direction, not understanding what was going on. The red dart lay deep in the tiger's side as she growled. The cubs yipped as they tumbled on each other, oblivious to what had just happened.

Now they had to wait for it to work. The tiger took a few steps as she let loose a string of growls, before her front legs gave way, then her back ones. She tumbled to the ground, her abdomen moving fast as she tried to catch her breath.

From experience, Charlee knew that she would have to wait a few minutes before approaching the tiger.

"Can we go now?" Alf asked. Excitement lined his voice.

"Hold on," Charlee murmured, holding up a hand as she watched the tiger through her rifle's lens.

They had to ensure that the medication would work. Nothing like walking up on a tiger who wasn't unconscious. That would be disastrous. They would have to wait for the signs of her breathing slowing by the movement of her abdomen.

Finally, the abdomen movement slowed to a steady pace. The tigress was officially unconscious.

"Now," Charlee announced to the group as she lowered her rifle.

Within minutes, the team broke from the brush and entered the clearing. West and Luka came from their area, still carrying their guns in their hand, but lowered as they approached.

Charlee had to beat down the excitement as she came upon the tigress. Her trained eyes examined her, and found her to be perfect. Her coloring of orange with black stripes, massive head and paws, left Charlee breathless. She sat her medical bag down so she could quickly examine the feline. The team had to be quick.

Zhang guided the graduate students to the cubs as they examined them. She could hear him teaching as they measured and played with the cubs. Zhang was a great professor and excellent educator. Charlee had been lucky to work with him a few times over the years. She made a note to herself to invite him to the university for a guest lecture. She knew that he would do it.

After they had all the documentations, measurements, and photographs that they would

need, Luka quickly went back over the microchips. He helped the team insert them in the scruff of the necks of the tigers. It was as easy as he'd initially described, like giving a flu shot. The tigress would wake up, not even knowing that she had been tagged. After they had ensured that all the chips were in, he showed them on the tablets how the tiger would be registered on the computer program.

"Once we leave and are at a safe distance, I can go back over the program," he said as they began gathering their supplies.

"This will be revolutionary," Dr. Zhang noted. "With the cubs, we can track their growth and where they migrate."

"Exactly. And they won't even know that they have something in them that broadcasts their location," Luka advised the group.

Charlee gave one more pet to the tigress as she stood. She couldn't stop the grin from spreading across her face as they all began making their way back to the forest. She glanced back one last time and caught a glimpse of the cubs wrestling again near their momma.

Once the team was at a safe distance, they would watch over the sleeping momma and cubs until she woke up. They didn't want to leave the cubs unprotected. Charlee couldn't wait to get back to the base to go through everything from today. She

couldn't believe how quickly they had found their first tiger. This trip was turning out better than she had expected. She glanced around and her eyes caught West's.

Much better.

ELEVEN

Laughter filled the air as the group gathered around the fire pit. Someone had gathered logs from the wood pile and put them around the pit. It was a gorgeous night. West watched as Charlee and the others talked animatedly about today's events. Luka glanced at him as the question came up on how they distracted the tiger.

"I mean, it sounded like another tiger was in the area," Malena scoffed, throwing her hands in the air.

"I know," Alf agreed. "That was weird. I kept expecting another tiger to jump out of the trees or something."

West's eyes met Luka's from across the roaring fire as everyone wanted to know how they distracted the tiger.

"I don't know what to tell you," Luka joked, taking a sip from his bottled water.

West and Luka knew the truth. Drago had been nearby in his cat form and provided the distraction for them. He had been keeping a close eye on the female tiger to ensure that the poachers hadn't returned.

The group had gone back to their spots when they first observed the tiger to ensure she was safe. Less than an hour later, the tiger sat up, a little dazed, but okay. After ensuring she was okay, the group returned back to their vehicles.

"It will remain a mystery," West murmured as he finished the last of his sandwich. He glanced at Charlee as she shared a log with Malena. They were engaged in a discussion with Dr. Zhang and his graduate student, exchanging information and ideas.

He was impressed by Charlee and her handling of a rifle. He guessed he shouldn't be. In her chosen career, traipsing around the world to study one of the most dangerous animals on the planet, one should know how to use a weapon.

"So where to next, Mr. Rogavac?" Dr. Skobo asked. West picked up on the slight hint of sarcasm that laced the scientist's voice. West glanced at the

Russian, and again that feeling in his stomach became noticeable. West leaned toward always listening to his gut, and in this instance he would. He knew that he would have to keep an eye on the Russian scientist. Something about him didn't sit right with West.

"I was planning to have us go a little more south. According to Dr. Zhang, there have been sightings of the Amur tigers in China." West gazed at the scientist, daring him to challenge the decision. Dr. Zhang had mentioned it to him earlier that he thought that would be the best place to go, and West agreed. It was also where evidence of poaching was the highest.

"That's a great idea." Charlee nodded. "I agree. I read your paper on this. How long have you suspected some of the Amur tigers have been migrating to China, and do they stay?"

West welcomed the change in conversation as Dr. Zhang answered Charlee's questions. He shifted on his log and gathered the remnants of his dinner, then went to toss it in the bag that was saved for trash. He looked up and noted the small moon. He knew that once the fire went out, the camp site would be cast in complete darkness.

Once everyone went to their separate tents to turn in, Luka would shift and guard the campground. They didn't want to let down their guard. As if hearing his thoughts, the scientists began to disperse,

all making excuses of tiredness and commenting about early starts tomorrow. He watched as Malena winked at Charlee as she walked to the tent that they shared.

Charlee stayed on her log as he returned. He moved toward her, his eyes locked on her smiling face as he approached. She had taken her hair down again. His tiger rumbled his pleasure in his chest.

He had to have her.

He sat down next to her, needing to be close to her. He reached up, no longer able to keep his fingers from her hair. The silky strands were soft against his fingers. The dwindling fire provided low light, highlighting her creamy skin.

"Hey there," she said softly. He glanced around and noticed that they were finally alone.

"Hey," he murmured, threading his fingers in her thick hair. He guided her to him, leaning his forehead against hers. He was trying to keep his shit together. The animal in him wanted to throw her over his shoulder and carry her off.

"So, I was wondering…" She paused, a small smile playing on her lips.

He pulled back. "What is it?"

"I was wondering when you would invite me into your tent," she breathed out, her eyes locked on his.

His tiger slammed into his chest. She didn't have to say another word. West stood quickly, grabbing her hand. They quickly put out the fire and kicked dirt on it to ensure that it was out. Without the fire, the campground was dark. A normal human wouldn't be able to see their hand in front of their own face, but thankfully for West, being a tiger shifter allowed him to navigate with ease in the dark.

Charlee remained quiet, her grip tightening on his as he stalked toward his tent. He was glad that he had bought the model that allowed for two people. He had contemplated when he bought it, and now he was so thankful to the salesmen who sold him the oversized two-sleeper.

They entered the tent and kicked their shoes off. He grabbed her by the nape of her neck and crushed his mouth to hers, needing to taste her again. Her hands found their way to his hair and gripped tight as the kiss transitioned to one of deep, urgent passion.

His hands slid beneath her T-shirt and pulled it over her head, breaking their kiss. She helped him out of his own shirt, leaving him bare. Her fingers trailed along his chest and down the ridges of his abdomen. Without light, his little human wouldn't be able to see, so she would have to learn his body by touch. He held in a groan as his cock pushed at his pants, demanding to be set free. She soon replaced her fingers with her mouth, trailing her tongue along his pectoral muscle to lavish his flat nipple with her warm tongue.

He reached around and undid her bra, sliding the straps down her arms. The soft feel of her skin beneath his hands had his mouth watering. He couldn't wait to taste all of her. They made quick work of their clothes in the small area before falling onto his sleeping bag.

She quickly shifted to allow him to settle within the valley of her legs. They both moaned as his cock brushed against her slick folds. He raised himself up slightly, not wanting to crush her with his weight. She met his kiss, inviting his tongue in. Her fingers dove into his hair as he trailed a line of kisses from her mouth, to the soft skin of her neck.

Her ample breasts pressed against his chest, as if seeking his attention. West couldn't leave them be. He had fantasized about them, and now he had them literally in the palm of his hand. He shifted down farther and captured one of her plump mounds into his mouth.

Their lovemaking remained quiet, but urgent, not wanting to draw attention to their activities. He wished they could let loose, but they couldn't, not tonight. This would not end once they left Russia and went back to the States. He would have her where he could hear her screams of passion.

Her short gasps drove his cat crazy. He moved to the other mound, dragging his tongue across the taut nipple before drawing it deep into his mouth. Her fingers tightened in his hair as he continued his discovery, moving even lower. In complete darkness, he knew that her senses would be heightened. He allowed his hands to trail along her skin as he moved. Her body released a shudder as he made it to his destination.

She hissed as he settled in-between her legs, eye level to her plump folds. He parted her lips and with his tongue, took one deep taste of her, running the flat of his tongue along the length of her slick pussy. He closed his eyes, relishing in the taste of her sweet nectar. Her legs spread even wider as he repeated the motion, before encircling her tiny nub with his tongue.

Her hips rose as he continued his gentle assault on her sensitive flesh. Her moisture coated his face as he continued to feast on her deliciousness. He pulled back on her clit before inserting one finger deep within her slick channel. Her inner muscles clamped down on his finger as he continued to maneuver her clit with his tongue. He increased the pace of his tongue against her sensitive nub as he moved his finger. Her legs shook as he inserted another finger, stretching her to prepare for him.

He increased the pace of his fingers, curving the tips of them. Her body jerked and her muscles tightened. Her silent orgasm caused her body to fly off the ground. He pushed her back down with one hand as he continued to suck on her clit. His cat was in heaven. Her creamy juices flowed right onto his tongue, causing his chest to rumble his pleasure.

Charlee's legs relaxed as he finally released her. He climbed over her body, his hardened length ready for her. West picked up her leg to open her more to him. His shifter sight could see that her eyes had opened. She reached up and grabbed him by the neck, crushing her mouth to his as he thrust deep within her, catching her moans.

A shudder passed down his spine at the feel of her moist core gripping his cock. Her pussy was slick from her orgasm, allowing him to slide into her with no problems. The kiss grew deep as his hips moved to their own rhythm. Not a word was passed between them. West was afraid if anything was to come out, it would be more of a yell or shout—not words.

The feel of her surrounding him was heaven. He squeezed his eyes tight as he quickened his pace. Her hips met his with every thrust. He opened his eyes to find her head thrown back as she let loose another gasp. He could feel her soft mounds rock with every thrust. He reached for one, needing to feel her breast in his hand as he continued to delve deeper into her core.

She wrapped her legs around his waist, pulling him deeper. Sweat broke out on his forehead as he felt the familiar twinges deep in his balls as they swayed and rhythmically slapped against Charlee.

He let her breast go to rest his arms on both sides of her head to get a better position to thrust deeper. He couldn't get enough of her, he had to get closer. She held onto his neck, bringing her head to the crook of his neck. She released a moan against his skin as her arm began to tremble, just as another orgasm took her over. She gently bit down on his skin, and that was enough to send him over the edge. He bit his lip to keep from shouting as he thrust harder, before pausing to release deep within her.

His breathing came fast and hard as he lowered his sweat drenched chest against hers. Both of them laid still, unable to speak. His cat was stiflingly quiet. It was content.

West knew one thing. This was just the beginning. No way was he giving up Charlee Black. She belonged to him.

TWELVE

"Spill it, woman," Malena demanded as she approached Charlee. She smiled, knowing that her best friend had been dying to get the details. But Charlee didn't know if she wanted to share what had occurred between her and West. They had made love into the wee hours of the morning, until she had to leave his tent. They both reluctantly got dressed and he escorted her back to the tent that she shared with Malena before anyone knew otherwise.

She didn't even have words for how she felt afterwards. She had laid down on her sleeping bag, still on cloud nine, with sleep nowhere to be found. Every inch of her body had tingled as she got lost in the memories, staring at the ceiling until the battery powered alarm went off.

"What are you talking about?" Charlee feigned innocence, as if she didn't know what her friend was talking about. She disconnected her camera cord from her laptop, then transferred the photographs she had taken to her computer to back them up. She didn't want to chance anything happening to her photos.

"Don't act dumb, woman." Malena stomped her foot. "I happen to know that you have a very high IQ, and there's not one dumb brain cell in your body."

"I think that was a compliment, so I'm just going to go ahead and say thank you," Charlee murmured, acting as if she was busy on her computer. While they had the generator and satellite connection, she needed to touch base with Alton and Jim.

"Don't you sit there and ignore me, Charlee Black. Inquiring minds want to know. I woke to you sneaking into our tent early this morning," Malena murmured, keeping her voice low as Alf and Tang, Dr. Zhang's assistant, walked past, deep in conversation.

Charlee looked up from her laptop and gazed around the temporary campground. Luka and Dr. Skobo were having a discussion, bent over one of the tablets. Zhang and West were leaning over one of the hoods of the truck with a map.

As if sensing her eyes on him, West looked up at that exact moment. She could sense the heat of his gaze across the distance. Her breath caught in her throat, and she was unable to look away from him. The memory of their night together was burned into her mind. She might as well have been blindfolded last night. It had been so dark in the tent, she was unable to see anything.

Only feel.

His hands and mouth had left her trembling. With only one look across the way, he had her core pulsating with need.

Cool down, girl, she thought to herself as she tore her eyes away from him.

"Mmm...yes, you need to spill all of the dirty, kinky details," Malena demanded as she stared at Charlee with one eyebrow raised. "Because that look you two just shared should be illegal. Spill it!"

"Okay," Charlee relented, turning to her friend. Malena scooted her foldable chair closer to Charlee, not wanting to miss any details. "If I tell you something, will you get back to work? We need to transmit information back to Jim and Alton."

"I sure will," Malena promised, drawing a cross on her chest. Charlee laughed at the excitement on her friend's face as she waited for Charlee to spill the beans. She leaned in so that they could speak without being overheard by one of the guys.

"Let's just say, the dry spell is over," Charlee admitted.

Malena released a squeal before slapping her hand over her mouth. Charlee laughed as Malena did a little dance in her chair. She could feel her cheeks redden with the memories. She wouldn't delve deeper, but she would at least put her friend out of her misery.

"I'm so happy for you. How was it? Earth shattering? As long as it's been for you, I sure as hell didn't hear any screams." Malena's words flew from her mouth quickly. Charlee held up her hand as she looked back across the campground, and found West's eyes on her again.

"Some things a girl has to keep to herself."

"You're such a tease," Malena groaned, falling back in her chair. "But seriously, girlie, I'm happy for you. Even if it's just a quick fling."

"I don't know about quick," Charlee admitted, turning to her friend. She didn't know if she would be able to leave and go back to the States without him.

"Do you have feelings for him?" Malena asked quietly, sitting back up. Charlee nodded, knowing that what had happened between her and West was a whirlwind, but deep in her heart, she knew she was falling for him.

Was she just a quick fling for him? They didn't talk relationship. They did talk about their families and learned about each other as they lied tangled together in each other's arms. But the word 'relationship' didn't come into the conversation.

Did she read last night wrong? Was she just a scratch to his itch?

West glanced again over at Charlee, unable to keep his eyes off her. The scientists continued to work over their computers and tablets as information was coming in from the ecologists and researchers' stations, leaving Charlee and her team to work frantically since they booted up the satellite's internet.

"So you and the good doctor?" Luka chuckled. West knew he couldn't lie to his friend. He was sure the scent of Charlee was still all over him. He didn't want to hide it either. He tore his eyes away from her and turned to his friend.

"Yes," he admitted with a straight face. Even though he wanted to strip and shift to allow his tiger to roar, he beat down those feelings and his animal. His animal wanted to lay claim to her, but it wasn't time for that yet. If he went about biting or scratching her with his claws, that would certainly scare her off. So he would have to hold him at bay until he could determine a better time to speak to her about a claiming.

"Good for you. She seems like a good match." Luka slapped him on the back. "Happy for you, man."

"Thanks," he said, a small smile gracing his lips.

Match.

She would be a great match. She was smart, intelligent, had a great job. And by the sounds of it, an amazing family.

West grabbed his satellite phone from his backpack and dialed Drago's number. It was time that he touched base with his security specialist. Tonight, he may not be able to shift and go off into the night to explore. If Charlee came to his tent, he would have to be there. There wouldn't be any way he could explain his disappearance into the woods in the middle of the night.

"Yeah," Drago growled into the phone.

"It's me. We've made it to the new location," West announced. "Anything we should know about?"

"We're not too far from you. Keep your eyes open at all times," Drago warned.

"What have you found?"

"There's evidence of poachers in the area. No new kills noted, but there is certainly evidence of them. We've found areas used for camps and tracks from vehicles that shouldn't be in here," Drago informed him.

"According to Dr. Zhang, there's proof that some of the tigers have began migrating to China." West relayed the information the Chinese scientist had shared with him.

"Interesting. But I have something even better to tell you," Drago growled. West went on alert instantly, sensing that something was off.

"What else have you found?" West glanced at Luka and saw the concern in his eyes as he waited for West to get off the phone.

"We found the remains of a human about twenty miles from your camp."

West released a curse and murmured to Luka what Drago had just shared with him.

"Go on," West commanded, wanting to know what else Drago had discovered.

"The man hadn't been dead long. I would say about a week or so. The thing is, he doesn't look like the poachers we ran into at the tigress' den. Those men were of Asian descent. This man wasn't."

"What are you thinking?" West asked, looking around the campground. Charlee and the scientists were still working. He turned his back to the group so he could pay close attention to what Drago had to say.

"My gut is telling me that this man had something to do with the shoot-out on the train. But I don't have proof. There are bullet casings everywhere. Something went down over here, and this man lost his life because of it."

West didn't like the sound of this at all.

"Stay close to us," West murmured.

His tiger paced beneath his skin at the thought of harm coming to Charlee. He couldn't take that chance. In the short amount of time since they had met, she had dug a hole in his heart. Fuck, she had her own personal chamber in it.

"Of course, sir."

West disconnected the call and turned back to Luka.

"How bad is it?" Luka asked, crossing his arms in front of his chest.

West shared with his longtime friend what Drago had informed him of, and Drago's gut feeling that the dead human was tied in with the train shooting.

"Fuck." Luka cursed as he took a few steps away.

"Yeah," West agreed.

The animal in him snarled as he glanced at the smiling Charlee. He wouldn't let anyone touch her.

They'd have to go through him to get to her. He would protect her with his last dying breath.

"We're going to tighten security around this research team and protect them. Something big is going on here in this sanctuary that someone wants kept quiet."

"I'll go out tonight and see what I can find," Luka volunteered.

"No, I'll go. I want you to get some rest tonight," West said. As much as he would love to spend another night in-between the soft thighs of Charlee, he had more pressing matters to attend to.

"Well, I won't turn down the opportunity to grab a few hours of sleep. Holler if you need me." Luka clapped him on the back.

"I'll be just fine."

THIRTEEN

West prowled around the perimeter of the campground as the humans slept. He went deeper into the forest to ensure that there were no imminent dangers. His cat, excited to be out again, took long strides as he put a lot of ground between him and the camp.

Charlee's face flashed before his eyes as he thought back to the gentle way he had to send her to her own tent tonight. Her soft smile and the twinkle in her eyes dimmed only slightly when he informed her that he would need her to sleep in her tent. He could tell that she was slightly confused. He promised her that he would explain later. He hated the feeling that filled his chest when she turned and walked away. His animal wasn't too happy either that she wasn't with them. She belonged in the tent with him.

Or better yet, his bed at home.

He didn't want to let on to the humans that there was danger on the horizon. Not yet. Not until he had to. It would cause a panic between the scientists if they thought their lives were in danger. They may pull back and leave, and he couldn't afford to have the mission aborted.

Finding and tagging the tigers was important. Almost as important as the ecologists discovering what was causing the tigers to migrate from the sanctuary. The dead human's body was proof enough that something was going on, and West and his men would get to the bottom of it. It was rare that West's gut led him astray. It was the main reason why they traveled around the world.

He knew back home that something was off about the sanctuary. Introducing the new microchips was the red herring. Yes, they wanted to go public with them and begin using them, but that could have been done at any time. Hearing that the Russian government was bringing in the top specialists to study the terrain and the animals in the sanctuary was the perfect opportunity for him and his men to get onto the grounds.

When the sanctuary was first open, SPAT was heavily involved, and still to this day were heavy financial contributors to the national park. But lately, there were too many discrepancies in reports that were sent to the SPAT offices. Reports of the poached tigers were inaccurate. It was as if the local government was trying to hide something.

The first day, when the Russian officials tried to insinuate that his presence was not needed, was another red flag. He instantly knew that the only men he could count on to take care of the poachers were his.

His tiger, distracted by an animal scurrying away, wanted to give chase, but West had to rein it in.

No chasing animals tonight, he informed his tiger.

He continued on his mission, creating a wide perimeter around the camp. A smell that was out of the ordinary to the thick rainforest caught his attention. Usually, tigers didn't use their noses for hunting, but this smell was so out of place that he couldn't help but stop and try to find where it was coming from. He crept around, moving the brush with his massive paw in search for the offensive smell.

Bingo.

A crushed cigarette butt. A few of them were gathered in one area, as if one person stood in place while they smoked and observed something

Or someone.

West looked around the dark forest floor and found a footprint on the dirt ground. Even in the dark, with his keen shifter eyes, he was able to follow the trail. Anger mounted in his chest as he realized where it led.

Back to the camp.

His paws picked up speed as he stalked through the rainforest, barely making any sounds. Tigers were known for their stealth, and it was no different for a shifter. He paused about twenty feet away from the forest edge, not wanting to take the chance that one of the scientists or assistants were out of their tents. It would cause a panic if it was known that a tiger had almost entered the camp.

He glanced down and found another cigarette butt on the ground. He looked up, and with his shifter eyes, he could see directly though the brush, and directly at Charlee's tent.

Someone was watching her.

His tiger hissed at the thought.

A noise coming from behind him caught his attention, as if someone was running. West took off in the direction of the noise. His cat took long strides as it raced through the dark. His tiger, in its natural habitat, was able to maneuver through the dense rainforest.

He leapt over a fallen tree, landing silently. He paused, no longer able to hear the person. He crept silently, searching for a sign of the mystery person. He was sure it was human and not an animal. He caught sight of a print in the mud.

Human tracks.

He took off faster, tracking the person, but another sound alerted him that another animal was in the area.

Chuffing.

He paused mid-stride and paused.

There it was again. Another tiger was in the area, and this one was familiar.

Drago's large tiger appeared before him and slowed, making his way out of the dense brush. The air around him shimmered as he slowly morphed into his human form. West followed suit, needing to speak with the security specialist.

"Someone was here," West began as he stood to his full height. Both of them were completely naked. Due to the shift, their clothes would be shredded, so when the shift was planned, a shifter would dispense of their clothes first. Nudity was second nature to them.

"I know. We were tracking him and found that they had been to the camp," Drago said, folding his arms across his chest. "I think they saw your tiger and got spooked, then ran off."

"He was coming this way," West snapped. He looked around, frustrated. "You're telling me that you didn't see anyone run in this direction? Whoever it was, was headed this way."

"This way? No, no one has been this way. We were making our way closer to the camp, following his tracks."

"I was following his tracks away from that area." West pointed in the direction he had just come from. How did humans just disappear into the middle of a rainforest?

"Well, whoever it was, they're far more familiar with the area then we are," Drago noted, his eyes perusing around the trees that surrounded them. "There are a million places for someone who knows the area to hide. We would never find them."

"Well, we need to. Whoever it was, was posted too close to Charlee's tent. Cigarettes lined the area, meaning they had been there a while. I want them found," West snapped, the alpha in him coming to the forefront. Drago's eyes dropped to the ground in submission.

"Yes, sir." Drago nodded.

"This is getting too close. We cannot afford for the humans to get spooked, pack up, and abandon the project."

"I sent Gerald to one of the secluded villages on the outskirts of the park near Kazakhstan," Drago informed him.

"What did he find?" West growled, trying to keep his tiger at bay. It prowled beneath his skin, ready to be free again.

"The villagers admitted that strange men had been there a few days before. Men with strange accents, asking questions about the tigers. When he asked the villagers if they seemed like common poachers, they laughed at him," Drago said.

"What would be so funny about that? They're the locals, they would know who poachers were," West said, confused.

"Exactly." Drago nodded. "They told Gerald that the men were certainly not poachers, but were bad men."

West growled. He was sure that they were the men from the train.

"Find them," he snapped. Turning his back, he walked into the brush, shifted, and took off, back toward the camp.

* * *

"What's going on?" Charlee murmured as she and Malena exited their tent. It was the wee hours of the morning, time for them to begin their hike for the day. Dr. Skobo's angry voice carried through the air.

"I don't know. Something must be wrong," Malena said, concern lining her voice as they walked toward the men where they gathered near one of the Land Rovers. That was where they walked up on a one-sided shouting match with Dr. Skobo and West.

"What's going on?" Charlee asked, looking around as she came to stand beside Dr. Skobo. His mouth snapped shut, and his face was beet red as he turned to Charlee. Her eyes turned to the very silent West. His solemn look was downright scary. His eyes burned with anger, and if it spilled over, she would be afraid for Dr. Skobo's life.

The look he shot Dr. Skobo was one of an angry predator. She noticed it again, that slight look that reminded her of a tiger. She shook her head and blinked as Dr. Skobo burst out with an explanation.

"Someone slashed the tire to the truck!" Dr. Skobo shouted.

"What?" Charlee gasped as she moved to the vehicle. Her eyes took in the mangled tire, and noticed how the truck leaned to the side. Whoever did it had to have had a large knife to be able to cut through such a large tire. "But why are you yelling at West?"

"It's because of him that we don't have the Russian guards that Mr. Yakovich assigned. He's put us in direct danger," Dr. Skobo shouted again, pointing his finger in West's face. Murmurs floated in the air at the accusation.

"Get your finger out of my face or you'll lose the whole fucking hand," West snapped.

"I'm sure there's a good enough reason," Charlee proclaimed.

"Go ahead, ask him," Dr. Skobo scoffed, waving his hands in the air.

She turned to West. Deep in her heart, she was sure if he did refuse the Russian's security, it had to be for a good reason. She would like to think that she was a good judge of character. In the short time she had come to know West, she knew him to be honorable. Her eyes searched his and found the truth in them. There was a reason he didn't want the Russian security with them.

"West, why did you turn down the security team?" she asked softly. Everyone in the group turned their eyes to him, waiting for his answer.

"I don't trust the Russian government right now," he stated, shooting a look at Dr. Skobo.

"That is absurd!" Dr. Skobo scoffed. "What kind of vague answer is that?"

"I have my reasons," West announced to the group, looking everyone in the eye. Charlee believed him, and knew that in good time, he would tell them. "It's for reasons you wouldn't understand."

"Of course. And we're all supposed to just believe you?" Dr. Skobo snapped.

"I believe you," Charlee told West.

"Of course you do. You're sleeping with him!" Dr. Skobo shouted. Charlee blanched at the scientist's words. She could feel the heat reach her cheeks as embarrassment flooded her.

A growl came from West as he jumped at the Russian scientist, but Luka grabbed him, holding him in place. The murderous look that crossed his face left little doubt of what would have happened if he got his hands on him.

West spat something in Russian at the scientist as he fought to get free from Luka's strong hold.

She was a grown woman. Her and West were two consenting adults, and they could do whatever they wanted. It was none of anyone's business what went on between them after hours when they weren't working on research. Charlee held her head high and turned to the scientist. Her open hand slap across his face stung her hand, but it was well worth it.

Dr. Skobo turned to her, and without a word, brushed past her and left the group. Charlee stood in place, unable to believe that she'd dared hit another scientist. Her body literally trembled from the shock of what just occurred.

"Let's get ready for the day." Malena's voice appeared next to Charlee as she encouraged everyone to gather what they would need for the trip. Murmurs filled the air as the others walked away.

"Are you okay?" West asked, standing in front of her. His fingers gently tipped her chin up, bringing her eyes to his. Just the slightest touch from him calmed her nerves. Concern burned in his eyes as he looked down at her. She nodded quickly, relaxing slightly as he brushed her hair from her eyes. "Don't worry about that ass. Let me handle him."

"Okay," she whispered. His eyes searched hers as he grabbed her hand and placed a gentle kiss in the middle of her palm. "What did you say to him in Russian?"

"Don't worry about it. Do you trust me?" he asked. She didn't even hesitate in her answer.

"Yes."

FOURTEEN

After the men changed the tired on the truck, the group was finally able to leave and began looking for another tiger. The tire certainly caused a delay, but luckily, the actual changing of the tire didn't take too long. They were only a couple hours behind schedule.

They were deep into the rainforest, miles from their campground. Charlee wiped the back of her hand across her forehead and found it to be covered with sweat. The humidity was increasing as the morning progressed. She paused to grab her water bottle from her backpack and took a quick swig before replacing it back in her pack.

West and Luka guided the group once again, using their fancy GPS technology that assisted them as they plunged deeper into the rainforest, until they finally reached the mountainous regions of the national park. The next few days would be pure roughing it in the elements on the side of the Altai Mountains.

She glanced off in the distance and her breath caught in her throat at the scenery that came into view. The perfect green valleys and rolling hills carved into the mountains were absolutely stunning.

"It's a thing of beauty," Malena breathed, as she too was in awe.

"I love my job," Charlee announced as a smile spread across her face.

She paused, knowing that she needed to get the shot. She moved to the side to allow the others to walk around her. She knelt down and grabbed her camera from a compartment in her backpack, and popped the cap off the lens. Peering through the lens, she focused her shot and immediately began snapping photographs. All around them was life. Undisturbed nature at it's best. Her heart swelled with the knowledge that with her help, the tigers would come back, and hopefully be a thriving species in the wild again.

"I told you I could get you the perfect shot," West whispered in her ear. She lowered the camera and turned to him, with a small smile on her lips. His eyes darkened as they glanced down at her. His intense look immediately took her breath away. She looked ahead and watched the last of the group continue on without them. His warm arms encircled her body, bringing her back against his firm chest.

"I've been wanting to feel you in my arms all day," he murmured against the back of her head. "Don't let me stop you."

She turned back, raising her camera again, but this time, she couldn't concentrate with his arms surrounding her. Just the feel of him had her wanting to strip his clothes off and have her wicked way with him. She turned her head, finding a magnificent looking bird pushing off from a tree branch. She captured the photo perfectly, just as the bird disappeared off into the distance.

Her breaths came in short gasps as he pushed into her from behind, bringing his hardened length in direct contact with the swell of her ass. She pushed back against him, and his chest rumbled with pleasure. Her pussy pulsed with the thought of the night they had shared, and any future nights.

"What kind of bird was that?" he asked, his voice low as he trailed his hand across her abdomen.

Her head fell back against his chest as his right hand disappeared into her khaki shorts. She closed her eyes, enjoying the feel of him surrounding her. She inhaled and breathed in his scent. He was all masculine. It was like the smell of him was an aphrodisiac. His fingers dove underneath her panties and continued their journey south.

"I don't know," she gasped as his fingers parted her plump lips, exposing her suddenly swollen nub. She could feel herself grow moist as his finger gently began to rub her sensitive nub. She bit her lower lip as he pinched her clit between his two fingers, before soothing it with just one finger.

"Go ahead, take your pictures," he murmured in her ear as he gently nipped on her lobe, leaving a trail of open mouth kisses on her neck. She released a moan as he continued his tortuous assault. She opened her eyes and tried to focus, but his hand and mouth were delicious distractions. She glanced around and found them totally secluded, yet on edge of the hill. The world was their audience.

She brought her camera up to try to find another shot, but her eyes closed again with the feel of his fingers dipping farther into her core. His fingers pulled her wetness from her center back to her clit and increased their speed. Her hips began to move in tandem with his fingers. She wanted—no, needed more.

"West," she gasped, her core pulsating, needing to feel him inside of her. "Please."

What she was asking for, she didn't know. Please stop? Hell no. Please have your way with me right here on the rainforest floor?

Definitely.

His other hand came up and cupped her breast through her shirt and squeezed. Her sensitive mound ached to have his hands on her bare breasts. She held onto her camera tight, afraid that she would drop the damn thing. If she did, the feel of his fingers on her pussy would be well worth it. Her other hand reached up and grabbed onto the back of his neck, in need of something to support her. Her heart raced from the sensations that swept over her. It was enough to send her tumbling down the hill face-first.

"Open your eyes." His deep voice caused her body to tremble. She complied and looked out at the world, just as he pinched her nub again, causing her orgasm to slam into her. She cried out as her muscles tightened, the waves of her orgasm crashing into her. His arm caught her as her legs gave out. He held her up against him as she shook from the sensations that coursed through her.

They stood there, both breathing heavily. She let go of his neck, shocked that she just had one of the hardest orgasms while in the rainforest for anyone to see. Thankfully, with them being in the rainforest, that chance was slim.

"Oh my," she murmured as he slowly removed his hand from her shorts. She turned and leaned into him, resting her forehead against his chest, still trying to catch her breath. West wrapped his arms around her body that still trembled, and she was sure that her legs had grown weaker.

What the hell has he done to me? she thought to herself with a short laugh.

"We better catch up with the others." West's voice broke through her orgasm fog.

"I'm not sure my legs will work." Her voice was muffled against his chest.

His chest shook with his laughter. He tipped her head back and covered her mouth with his. A moan escaped her as she leaned into the kiss, loving the feel of his tongue wooing hers.

He pulled back and placed another chaste kiss upon her lips.

"That was just a preview. There will be more later. I promise you this."

The smell of Charlee remained on his hand and he loved it. The cat in him wanted him to lick his fingers to get a taste of her, but he resisted. His cock had yet to go down. It took everything in him not to strip their clothes off, push her up against one of the trees and plunge his cock deep inside of her, and fuck her until neither of them could walk.

One time was not enough, he needed to have her again. His tiger would not rest until they could be sated inside of her once more. He should have never touched her when they were on the hill. It was a tease, and left him even more sexually frustrated.

The group had finally made it to a safe destination where they could set up and wait to see if they could find one of the tigers that had been tagged before with the old tags. According to the paperwork that was given about some of the tigers, this one was one that had been caught as a young tiger when it was injured and re-released into the wild. The tiger was named Bubo by the humans who had cared for him.

Bubo was known to gravitate toward the side of the mountains, according to the records. There were multiple satellite photos of the tiger in the area. West knew if they didn't catch sight him today, then Luka would shift and go looking for the tiger to get a heads-up on his location.

West leaned back against his tree and watched Charlee as she worked. Tensions were still high with Dr. Skobo. West was still proud of Charlee for sticking up for herself. Dr. Skobo got off with just that slap. Had Luka let West go, he would have surely did major damage to the scientist.

"I've spoken to Drago," Luka said, dropping down next to West.

"And?" West didn't take his eyes off Charlee. She was certainly in her element. She was speaking with the graduate students, and they were just as captivated by her. He could see from where he was perched that she loved all aspects of teaching.

"One of his men are keeping an eye on the campground while we're on the mountain," Luka said.

"Good." He nodded, watching her laugh at something that Tang said. Her smile was infectious, and neither student could resist smiling along with her.

"Is it serious?" Luka's voice interrupted his thoughts.

"What?" He turned to his friend, not understanding his question. He found Luka staring at him with a small smile on his lips.

"You and the doctor? I asked if it was getting serious." Luka chuckled. "I don't think you've heard one thing I've said since I sat down. Your attention is totally consumed by her."

"I heard you," West scoffed. He wasn't that bad. Luka had him sounding like a love starved cub with a crush. "I don't know."

His eyes turned back to Charlee, and he knew he wouldn't want to be with anyone else. His tiger snarled at the thought of not having her in their lives. He was becoming possessive of her.

Could she be the one?

FIFTEEN

Charlee peered through her binoculars, but didn't see any signs of Bubo. It had been one whole hour since she had climbed into the tree in hopes of spotting him.

"I think we should call it a night," Dr. Zhang called up to her from the base of the tree. He was right. If they needed to spend the night on the mountain, then they would. It was imperative that they tag as many tigers as they could during their month-long stay.

"I'm coming," she called out as she began to shimmy down the tree. It was getting late, and soon darkness would be upon them. The team had separated within a mile radius of each other, in hopes of finding some sign of the tiger. They wanted to identify the area that the tiger would be, instead of just walking up on it. But so far, no signs.

She made it down to the bottom of the tree. Zhang helped her unhook her harness as she stepped out of her safety rope. They disassembled the set up from the tree in silence. Her mind raced a mile a minute. Zhang, ten years her senior, was someone whose opinion she held in high regard. He was someone that she respected and looked up to. They had worked together multiple times on papers, and she didn't want to chance losing his respect. Dr. Skobo's accusation rang in her ears, and she knew that she had to say something.

"Hey, Zhang," she said, grabbing his arm as they began the walk back to the group.

"Yes, Charlee?" he asked, surprise lining his face as he stopped.

"Look, about earlier—"

"There's no need to explain," he said, holding up his hand. He barked out a laugh and patted her hand. "You and Mr. Rogavac are grown adults. As long as everything is consensual, I don't see anything wrong with it."

"I still need to apologize. It's unprofessional to mix business with pleasure. I just want you to know that this mission is very important to me," she said, pushing an annoying strand of hair from her eyes.

"We've known each other for years. Just because Skobo is an ass, doesn't mean you should feel bad for what goes on when you're not working. You are a brilliant biologist. Don't let one person's stupidity bother you."

Relief spread through Charlee. She was worried that the others would change their opinion of her.

"I just don't want anyone to think of me as anything else but a scientist," she admitted as they began walking back to where the group was to meet.

"Charlee, no one thinks differently of you. But you want to know what?" he asked, eyebrow raised.

"What's that?" she asked, adjusting her backpack.

"You are a woman first, and a scientist second. Don't ever forget that. And if it makes you feel any better, I met my wife on a trip similar to this one about fifteen years ago. We've been together ever since. It's just the nature of our business."

"Really? I didn't know that." She laughed, relaxing more as they arrived at their destination. Others were arriving, coming from different directions. "Thanks, Zhang. I really appreciate it."

"No problem." He saluted her as he made his way over to his graduate student.

Charlee turned and caught West's eyes as he emerged from the trees with Luka behind him. Her

heart did a little pitter-patter as he winked at her. She smiled, gave a small wave, and walked over to Malena. If she would have stood there longer to stare at him, she wouldn't have been able to stop herself from launching herself at him. It was much safer for her to go over to Malena.

"Any luck?" Charlee asked Malena, who was speaking with Alf.

"We think we found a few tracks, but we're losing light. We marked the tree where we found them. We'll be able to check them out in the morning," Malena said, looking up at the sky.

With their late start and long travel times, it didn't leave much time for them to find the tiger. They would have to camp out tonight, then get an earlier start. They wouldn't dare go looking for a tiger in the middle of the night in the rainforest. That would be too dangerous.

"Good thinking for marking the tree." Charlee nodded her head. She dropped her bag down and plopped on the ground next to Malena. She was tired, hot, dirty, and famished. She grabbed her bag and searched for one of her protein bars. She snagged one and practically devoured it whole after fighting with the wrapper.

"You might want to chew a few times," Malena laughed. Charlee tossed her wrapper at her friend with a chuckle. She couldn't help it.

Today was a bust. Someone sabotaged their vehicles. It was announced that she slept with someone in the group, and then no tiger. Charlee was ready for this day to end. Her sleeping bag was calling her name, and she couldn't wait to grab a few hours of sleep. She hoped tomorrow would prove to be better. They would find Bubo, tranq him, gather as much data as they could, then insert the microchip in him.

"Can I speak to everyone, please?" West announced, waving everyone over to the center of the clearing.

Charlee groaned with the thought of getting up from her seat. Her body was beginning to stiffen up from the exertion of walking up the side of a mountain. Malena laughed and dragged her to a standing position. Everyone gathered near West. Charlee avoided looking over at Dr. Skobo. She could feel his eyes on her, but she had nothing else to say to him. They were here to do a job, and that's exactly what she would do. She was a damn good scientist, and whatever this was between her and West would not interfere with that.

"Tonight, we'll be sleeping in the open. Because we're on the side of mountain, we will need to rotate people throughout the night to keep watch. We need to make sure that no hungry animals come crashing into on our camp."

"I'll take first watch," Luka volunteered, raising his hand.

"Thanks, and I'll relieve you after a few hours." West nodded his head. "Let's grab something to eat and hit the sack. We'll have an early morning tomorrow."

Silence filled the air, except for a few snores. West was restless and unable to sleep as thoughts of Charlee filled his mind. His tiger was restless too. It knew they were in the jungle, and he wanted to be let free so that he could roam the humid forest. He stood silently and wandered over to the end of the camp. Luka leaned back against a tree and nodded when his eyes met West's.

The fire in the pit in the middle of the clearing had finally dwindled to just smoldering embers. He glanced to where Charlee should have been sleeping, but found her bedding to be empty. His eyes shot to Luka and found his friend pointing to a place behind him. He turned and found Charlee emerging from the trees.

"I needed to use the facilities," she murmured, a sheepish look coming over her face.

He chuckled as he walked toward her. His tiger paced back and forth with the knowledge that she was close. Her hair, piled on top of her head, had his fingers itching to remove the bun. He wanted to see her thick locks spill out onto her shoulders and back.

He grabbed her hand and entwined his fingers with hers.

"Walk with me," he murmured. Her face softened as she nodded her head. He looked over his shoulder at Luka to see him give a small salute. He pulled her behind him as they entered the dense wooded area.

"How can you see?" she asked, bringing her other hand to rest on the small of his back as he led her farther away from the others. His eyes quickly adjusted to the darkness of the forest. The sounds of nature greeted them as they continued to walk.

"There's a little moonlight," he murmured, making an excuse. There was no way he could tell her the truth. He kept them moving, knowing exactly where he wanted to take her. He had discovered a beautiful little cove that would be perfect for them to have time alone, and he couldn't wait to get her there.

He knew that Charlee was in love with everything about the rainforest, and his tiger was pleased by this. Every new discovery, her camera wasn't far from her hands. Her appreciation of what nature had to offer was evident by her passion, in not only preserving

the tigers, but in everything he had come to know that she stood for.

"Where are we going?" She released a nervous chuckle. His animal could pick up that she was a little antsy. His thumb drew small circles on her inner wrist in an attempt to calm her nerves.

"It's a surprise," he announced. "I found something earlier that I wanted to share with you."

"Oh, shoot. Maybe I should have grabbed my camera," she said.

"Don't worry—" The sound of a twig snapping grabbed his attention. His tiger instantly went on alert. He hadn't picked up on the trail any other animals in the area. Charlee instantly sensed that something was wrong. His body drew tense as he waited and listened, willing his heart to slow down.

"What was that?" she whispered. The smell of her fear permeated the air.

He held a finger up to his lips as he turned to her, not sure if she was able to see the motion. He listened again, and another snap echoed through the air. His head snapped in the direction of the noise, and he pushed Charlee behind him. He could feel both of her hands on the small of his back. His ears perked up as he waited.

His eyes met those of a tiger, peering out of the trees fifty feet from them. His amber eyes glowed in the dark as he assessed West and Charlee.

"Oh my God," Charlee gasped, having peeked from behind him.

"Stay behind me," he ordered, pushing her back. His tiger pushed forward with a roar as they stood there and stared down the tiger.

The tiger nodded his head, and West released the breath he didn't know he had been holding.

Drago.

Drago's tiger disappeared back into the trees without a sound. West knew that Drago had caught sight of Charlee and would give them privacy, and also ensure that no other dangerous animals were in the area.

"He's gone," West murmured, holding still to make sure Drago had left.

"Was that Bubo?" she asked, eyes wide. Her grip tightened on his hand.

"I'm not sure," he lied, pulling her behind him. "It could have been. But I'm sure you know that tigers can be shy animals. He's probably moving through the area.

"Maybe we should try to follow him. He could lead us to his den—"

"No." He held up a hand to cut her off. "We are not following a tiger in the middle of the jungle at night. Smart people like ourselves will keep on moving and put as much distance between us and a tiger who could eat us whole."

"Oh, yeah. I guess you're right. I just got excited," she laughed. Her excitement over tigers was infectious. He ached to be able to share his other half with her. His tiger would love to have the feel of her hands on his head and rubbing between his ears.

Not yet, he snapped to his tiger, pushing his animal down. It was too soon. His tiger scoffed at the notion of waiting. He was getting impatient, and it was taking a lot of energy to keep his tiger at bay.

"Here we are."

SIXTEEN

"Oh my goodness, West. It's beautiful," Charlee gasped. She clasped her hands to her chest as she took in the beautiful serene picture that was in front of her. "How did you find this place?"

She stared at the small private spring that was surrounded by lush tropical plants. Steam rose from the water. Right above the small spring, the sky was open. It was like the Gods had parted the trees just to cast moonlight directly over the small pool of water.

It was downright romantic.

Her breath caught in her throat as she took it all in. Her eyes made their way to West, and her heart slammed into her chest. His look was intense as his eyes bored into hers. It was amazing how one look from this man had her pussy weeping, as if to prepare itself for him. She turned to him as he reached up and pulled her hair, releasing it from the messy bun.

"We came across this when we all separated into pairs. Luka and I found this when we were searching for Bubo. I knew you would love it."

"It's almost magical," she whispered, not tearing her eyes away from his dark ones.

With the moonlight casting down on them, she could make out the stubble on his jaw. Her fingers instantly reached for him, needing to feel the scruffiness of his jaw. There was something about his rugged look that made her core clench with need.

"Swim?" he murmured, running his fingers through her hair.

Unable to speak, she nodded her head. He snagged the bottom of her shirt and pulled it over her head. She returned the favor, excitement rising to finally see him in the light. Their one night of lovemaking had been in complete darkness. She had no complaints from that night. None at all. But this time, she would get to see everything that she experienced.

The ridges of his abdomen came into sight and her knees weakened. Her arousal grew as she ran her fingers down his chest, needing to feel him. She wouldn't be able to find an ounce of fat on this man if she tried. His quick intake of breath let her know that she affected him as much as he did her.

Her fingers continued their way down to his pants where she quickly unbuttoned them. She held in her breath as he guided the zipper down. He waited patiently as she disrobed him. It was like he was allowing her to slowly open a Christmas gift.

Only this was the best damn gift she had ever had the pleasure of opening.

She pushed his pants down, kneeling in front of him to assist him in kicking them off. His large bulge was eye level to her. She licked her lips as she ran her hand along his covered member, teasing a moan from him as she reached for the edge of his boxer briefs. She successfully hooked her fingers beneath the edge and brought his underwear down in the same fashion as his pants, freeing his enlarged cock. Weston Rogavac was a blessed man. He was stiff, hard, and ready for her.

Unable to hold back, she caught the tip of his bobbing member between her lips without even using her hands. He groaned as she reached up and gripped the base of his length as she guided it deeper into her mouth. She stroked him as her tongue caressed the wide tip. She pulled back slightly, leaving just the tip in her mouth as she glanced up.

He stood in one place with his eyes closed, basking in the feel of her mouth wrapped around his cock. The expression of complete enjoyment was etched on his face, making the wetness seep out of her core. She slid him back in, not letting go, wanting to please him. She continued her delicious torture, loving the salty taste of him on her tongue. She increased the pressure from her hand, moving her head in a rhythm.

His hand reached down and threaded its way into her hair as he spread his legs wider for better balance. He gasped as she swallowed, bringing him farther into the back of her throat.

"Charlee," he murmured as she reached up with her other hand to cup his scrotum. She caressed his quivering sac with her fingers. Charlee knew that he was close. Her saliva spilled out of the open sides of her mouth, coating his cock, allowing it to slide easier between her hand and lips. She increased her rate again, along with the pressure, wanting to tip him over the edge.

His breaths came fast, and she watched as his abdomen muscles rippled.

Because of her.

She did this. She literally had him in the palm of her hands, and she loved how she could affect him

in the way that he did her. His grip tightened in her hair as he pulled her head back, amidst her small protest.

"No, not yet," he gasped, pulling her up to stand.

He quickly disrobed her, leaving them both naked beneath the moon. He lifted her behind her knees easily, as if she didn't weigh anything. His pure strength amazed her. She instinctively wrapped her legs around him. He crushed his mouth to hers as he walked directly into the warm water. He thrust forward, his thick cock surging into her. His mouth caught her groan. Their bodies were submerged in the warm spring as he walked farther into the water.

She wrapped her arms around his neck, crushing her breasts to his chest as he continued to devour her mouth. His hands gripped her plump ass as he pulled back and thrusted in again. He moved her body up and down his length. The slight burning sensation from her pussy walls being stretched felt so good. She broke the kiss with a gasp and buried her head into the crook of his neck. Her core spasmed, contracting on his cock as he continued to pound his length into her.

"West," she moaned as he filled her completely. They floated around in the water. It splashed around them as she rotated her hips and pushed down onto him. She needed him closer, more of him in her. She wanted to consume him. She didn't know why, but she had to have all of him. He growled as she nipped his shoulder with her teeth.

Her back hit the far wall of the spring. She let loose a cry as warm clay met her bare back. She moved her head and met the eyes of West as he growled, increasing the speed of their joining. His eyes flashed something feral and she knew that he was close. Only the sounds of their coupling and the light splashes of the water filled the air. She fisted his hair in her hand, needing something to hold on to.

She leaned in and met him for a hard kiss, their lovemaking turning more urgent. She clenched her inner walls on him, eliciting the sexy growl that she was starting to love to hear. Her breaths were coming faster as the surge of emotions rippled through her body.

"Come on, baby. You're almost there," he groaned against her mouth.

She was right there on the edge. He tipped her hips and thrust harder. At this angle, it brought his cock in direct contact with her sensitive nub. Her body trembled with each thrust. Her inner walls spasmed as she began to shake uncontrollably. She closed her eyes as his finger parted her plump lips beneath the water's surface, exposing her swollen nub.

She cried out, not caring who heard them. She dug her nails into his back as his thumb brushed against her clit, driving her over the edge into ecstasy. Her body tensed as the waves of her orgasm washed over her. His body trembled as he released a roar, shooting his release deep within her. He gripped both of her ass cheeks tight as he continued to thrust, spewing his release. She was sure that she would have bruises, but she could care less. It was totally worth it.

Neither of them moved. Her head dropped back down to the crook of his neck as she tried to catch her breath. His chest was rising just as fast as hers. The water around them calmed down as they remained still.

She never wanted to move from this position, with his cock comfortably snug inside of her. They could stay this way for all eternity for all she cared.

"Charlee," he murmured, reaching up to brush her soaked hair from her face.

"Mmm..." That was all she could formulate. No words would come to mind. She was a big ball of mush. Her arms were heavy, as they were still wrapped around his neck.

"I want you."

"You just had me." She barked out a laugh. She clenched her walls that surrounded him, feeling him growing hard again. She smiled against his wet skin.

"I'm serious. I want there to be an "us." I don't want things to end when we leave here to go back

to the States," he admitted. She leaned back at the serious tone in his voice. She was thankful for the moonlight. It allowed her to look at him and see that he was dead serious.

"Is Weston Rogavac asking me to go steady with him?" She was dramatic with her question, bringing the back of her hand to her brow. His face broke out into a smile as he chuckled. Her heart swelled with the knowledge that he wanted her.

"Yes, I am. I just want it to be you and me," he said, the smile fading from his face as he gazed deep into her yes.

"That sounds good to me."

"So where were you two coming from this morning?" Malena asked with accusing eyes. She wiggled her eyebrows as she waited for the answer.

Charlee groaned. She would have preferred someone else to catch them when they came back to the camp. Malena claimed she had woken up early to go pee and didn't see Charlee or West. Once everyone woke up, Charlee had tried to avoid her friend, but Malena was not having any of it.

This morning, they had finally picked up the trail of Bubo. His tracks were actually leading them back down the mountain. West and Luka had gone farther, requesting the team to set up and be ready. Charlee had her rifle in her hand as she waited.

"Malena, leave it alone. I told you he showed me a spring where I could get washed up."

"Uh-huh, and he didn't show anyone else. We all could have taken turns washing some of this rainforest dirt off. I swear, I'm so dirty that even the mosquitos don't want me."

Charlee rolled her eyes at her friend's dramatics. She glanced around the area, knowing that her friend would never let up. The guys were spread out, waiting for a sighting of the male tiger.

"Okay, if you must know..." She paused to create her own dramatics.

Malena's eyes grew round as she waited. Instead of verbalizing what she and West did at the spring, Charlee held up two fingers, symbolizing the second time that she and West had sex. But she didn't want to just call it sex. Something was exchanged between the two of them. It was even more than lovemaking, but she wouldn't tell Malena that. She wouldn't understand. She'd think that Charlee was a little touched in the head.

"We have movement." A low voice came across the small walkie-talkie.

Malena and Charlee both drew quiet as Charlee raised her rifle and stared out through the lens to wait, scanning the brush lower down on the mountain. From her perch, she had a perfect view of the mountain. A large tiger slowly ambled from out of the brush. It walked slowly, pausing every few steps, as if it sensed it was being watched. Charlee took aim and held her breath, willing her heart rate to slow. The tiger paused in walking and looked at something in the brush a hundred feet from him.

West.

It turned toward the noise, giving Charlee exactly what she needed. She pulled the trigger.

SEVENTEEN

Once the tiger was unconscious, the team sprang into action. Upon assessment of the tiger, they learned that it had a recent gunshot wound. Anger festered in West's chest at the thought of poachers being close by.

Even though Dr. Skobo and Charlee hadn't really spoken since the other morning, they worked silently together for the tiger, cleaning and assessing the wound.

"It went straight through," Charlee announced as she poured a solution on the tiger's wounded hind leg.

West stayed perched by the tiger, petting its massive head. West's eyes moved to Luka, and the same rage burned in his friend's eyes.

"Do you want me to give him a shot of antibiotics?" Dr. Skobo asked as he rummaged through his bag.

"That wouldn't be a bad idea," Dr. Zhang commented, as he and Malena finished inserting the microchip.

The graduate students were busy documenting into the tablets that would transmit information back to the research team that stayed behind.

"We need to hurry. The tranq will be wearing off soon," Charlee instructed as she began packing her bag back up.

West looked down at the massive orange and striped head beneath his fingers. His tiger snarled at the thought of poachers hurting this animal. Now with the new microchip, they would be able to track the tiger in real time.

The team was fast and proficient at getting everything they needed. They cleared out, and again, waited at a safe distance for the tiger to wake up. Once its massive head rose from the ground, West released his breath as he watched the tiger scamper off into the thick brush.

He walked over to Luka as the scientists celebrated another success. His tiger was close to the front and was demanding blood.

"This is getting too close," he growled, low enough where only Luka would hear him. "It's time we flush the poachers out. I want this over."

"I'll contact Drago to let him know what we found." Luka nodded before walking away.

It was still early enough for the group, so they decided to start making the trek down the mountain in order to make get back to the normal camp.

West was not in a good mood. He kept to himself, trying to contain his anger. Just the thought of the poachers being so close had him seeing red. He knew that they couldn't pinpoint exactly when Bubo was shot, but the wound was fresh. It had to have happened within the last day or two.

Murmurs of concern for the camp floated in the air. The conversation was about the other day when the tire was slashed. West was not going to tell the group that they'd had someone guarding the campground. Everything about Dr. Skobo kept doubt in the back of his mind. With the Russians questioning his reasons for being on the trip, he wouldn't tell any of them the real reason he was there.

To stop the poaching.

Knowing that the point of the sanctuary was to help the endangered species, they should provide some type of security for them. The cheap cameras he had seen mounted on this trip so far were a joke. He would bet most of them didn't even work. What was a camera to do but record what happened anyway? It was not a way to prevent poachers from walking or driving right into the national park, shoot a tiger in the head and drag its body off the property.

"Are you all right?" Charlee's soft voice appeared at his side. He glanced down at her and felt his heart soften. He nodded and grabbed her hand, entwining their fingers together as they walked. Just her sheer presence seemed to calm down his tiger. "I can see that you're upset about Bubo."

"Yeah." He blew out a breath and shifted his backpack higher on his back. "This place is supposed to be a safe place for the tigers so that they can re-populate. It pisses me off that people are so callous and want to kill an animal such as a tiger."

She squeezed his hand, not saying a word. She didn't need to. Just that outburst alone made him feel better. It didn't take away that his tiger wanted to break free and maul the poachers. Instead, his tiger just paced beneath his skin, waiting for the moment he would be able to break free.

The group continued on in silence, eventually making the few hour trip down the mountain and arriving safely at the camp.

"Everything looks the same," Dr. Zhang noted as they walked through it.

"Maybe it was just an animal that sliced the tire?" Malena suggested, looking around.

Murmurs echoed around as everyone shuffled to their tents. West looked around and saw a rustle of leaves off in the distance. It was probably Drago's man, Gerald, disappearing back into the woods. West's eyes met Luka's. He nodded in the direction, and Luka's eyes traveled over to the area and returned a nod as he made excuses and headed over, disappearing into the trees.

"I think I can just crash right now," Charlee said, her words ending in a yawn. "I'm beat."

"Go get some rest," he said, pulling her close and placing a kiss on her forehead. "We leave at first light," he announced, loud enough for the whole group to hear.

"Tomorrow, I have an idea of where we can go next," Dr. Skobo said, approaching them. West pushed Charlee in the direction of her and Malena's tent, hinting for her to go. He would deal with the Russian scientist. She hesitated for a moment, but she must have read the look in his eyes before walking away toward her tent. His eyes followed the

sway of her bottom that peeked from beneath her large backpack.

"Where do you think we should go next?" West asked, turning back to Dr. Skobo. He didn't hold the disdain from his voice.

Dr. Skobo produced a map and motioned for West to follow him over to one of the Land Rovers.

"This area of the sanctuary is known to be a hot spot for tiger sightings." He pointed to an area Northeast of where they were currently. It would take a few hours for them to get there.

"How do we know that?" West asked, studying the map more in-depth.

"From the cameras that are posted. They get multiple snapshots of different tigers in the area. There's a large watering hole in the area that is an attraction for all animals. It's a good place for them to hunt too, so it has a lot of action. I think that would be the best area to go next."

West nodded his head, silently agreeing with the scientist. If they wanted to be able to tag as many tigers as possible, it only made sense to go to a location that would attract them.

"Good plan," West said, his eyes catching Luka emerging from the woods. "Excuse me." He walked away toward his friend.

"We got a problem," Luka murmured, keeping his voice down as Dr. Skobo walked past them toward his private tent.

"What is it?" West asked as they moved toward where their tents were positioned.

"Gerald said that right before we came, a man came from the other side of the woods and placed a tracker on one of the Land Rovers."

West released a curse. "Are we sure it's a tracker?"

"Yes. He already checked it out and that's why he was just dashing back into he woods as we were arriving. He didn't get a chance to take it off. He'll do it tonight while everyone's asleep."

West shook his head. "No, leave them. This will be the best way for us to flush out the poachers, or whoever the fuck this is."

Luka growled low, his eyes flashing amber for a brief moment before transitioning back to his normal color. "They better show their faces."

"Don't worry. Our animals will be able to have fun with them when they show their faces."

West would have to say that Dr. Skobo was correct in his recommendation of them traveling to the Northeast region of the national park. With the park being over three hundred thousand acres, that meant they would have a lot of miles to cover. The watering hole had certainly paid off. In the past few days, they had inserted a microchip into two more tigers.

The team was in high spirits with the tigers that they had been able to study and gather data on. Charlee had all but moved into West's tent. He at first thought that she would be a little hesitant since she was around her colleagues, but she informed him everyone on was grown and could mind their own damn business. Everyone in the group seemed to accept it as well. Even Dr. Skobo quit making snide remarks. The Russian scientist even kept his mouth shut and did his job.

"We may have to go back to the main campground sooner than we thought," Charlee said, coming to sit next to West.

"Why is that?" he asked, turning to her.

"We're going to run out of tranquilizers soon," she offered, tucking an offending strand of hair behind her ear. "I guess it's a good thing that we're finding tigers so quickly. I have enough for a few more, but we'll need more if we keep finding them like we are."

He nodded his head. A few more days and he hoped that the traps they were setting up around the area would pan out. Nighttime was falling upon them, and they'd had a hard day. With being near a watering hole, there was an increased number of wild animals, not just tigers. Other animals that would be deemed just as dangerous.

They had to be on high alert to ensure that no animals wandered into their campground.

"I'm sure everyone would appreciate getting a real shower and food," West said with a chuckle, looking around the grounds as everyone settled in.

"Yes," she groaned, rotating her neck. "I would kill right now for a hot shower, fluffy white towels, and a big soft robe to wrap around me."

Her words brought a vision to his mind. He imagined her fresh from a hot shower, her skin still moist and rosy from the heat of the water. He imagined taking her into his arms and removing the towel—

He coughed and shook his head to erase the fantasy from his mind. He couldn't wait to get back to the States. What he had told her the other day was the truth. He wanted them to carry on at home. He didn't want this to be a quick fling in the jungle.

A loud curse filled the air, grabbing West's attention. Alf came storming out of his tent, frantically running his hands through his hair.

West jumped up and rushed over. He could feel Charlee behind him as they approached the still cursing and pissed off graduate student.

"What's going on?" West snapped, getting Alf's attention.

"It's missing!" Alf cried out.

"What's missing?" Charlee asked, a concerned look on her face.

"All of my handwritten notes. My notebooks that I was pulling together for my dissertation."

"Calm down and think. Did you take it with you today?" Malena questioned, coming to stand next to Charlee. The entire group surrounded them, curious as to what was going on.

"No, I haven't been taking these with me when we go out since we got here. I've been leaving it here in my tent since we've been taking the tablets."

"It has to be somewhere," Charlee said. "Has anyone seen them?" She turned to the group.

West's tiger stood at attention. No one here would have any reason to steal a graduate student's notes. They were all members of the research team, and would no doubt have their own records and notes.

His eyes met Luka's while a few of the team helped Alf search. It seems as if their stalkers had made their first move.

Let the games begin.

EIGHTEEN

"Can you believe it?" Malena asked, exasperated. "How do binders of notes just up and disappear?"

"I'm not sure," Charlee replied, feeling helpless for her graduate student. Losing notes for a dissertation was horrible. She didn't want to ask why he hadn't used a laptop for his notes. In his mental state right now, he would probably lose it.

"Someone had to have taken them," Dr. Skobo accused, looking around the group. His eyes stopped on the Chinese graduate student.

"Hey, it wasn't me,"Tang said, holding his hands up. "You can search my things if you'd like," he offered to Alf.

"No, I'm not going to search your things. I believe you." Alf sighed, resting his entwined hands on his head. Pure defeat was written on his face. Charlee felt sorrow for her student. She would have to sit down with him and go over the research they had already gathered to see if she could help salvage something for him. One day he would be a brilliant biologist, and she didn't want this to deter him from his dream.

Charlee and Malena turned to leave, but West requesting for everyone to gather around him kept them in place.

"I think we need to have a chat." He began. Everyone glanced at each other, unsure of what he was about to say. Charlee felt deep in her heart that whatever it was would be best for the group.

"In light of recent things that are going on, books don't just disappear. Tires don't just get slashed by random animals and no one hears it. I think it would be in everyone's best interest to pair up with someone when leaving the grounds. Even if it's to go in the woods to use the restroom. Let's err on the side of caution."

Murmurs of agreement filled the air.

"He's right," Dr. Zhang said, stepping in the middle of the circle. "We are in the middle of a rainforest in a mountainous region, where there is always danger lurking. We've been lucky not to have any injuries."

Charlee nodded in complete agreement. They had been lucky so far. They shouldn't test their luck. The small group began to disperse after their quick huddle.

"I need to pee," Charlee announced to Malena softly. "Will you be my buddy?"

"You sure West isn't your buddy?" Malena asked with a raised eyebrow. Ever since Charlee had made the move, Malena had found all kinds of ways to make fun of her. She turned, feeling West's eyes on her. She mouthed the word 'pee' and pointed to the woods. He nodded his head and went back to his conversation with Luka.

"Oh, cut it out." Charlee swatted her on the arm. They quickly ran over to the tent she shared with West to grab her biodegradable toilet tissue and headed into the woods. They decided not to go too far.

"This should be fine," Charlee announced, finding a spot that would block the view of her squatting. She finally got over everyone knowing that her and West were officially an item. Having one

of the guys catch her urinating would be another ball of wax. That would be hard to get over.

"What do you think really happened to Alf's work?" Malena asked as she turned her back to give Charlee privacy.

"I don't know. It's weird though. Who would steal his work? We all have access to the information that we've been collecting." Charlee quickly unbuttoned her pants and bent down to do her business. She closed her eyes with relief at the chance to finally be able to empty her bladder.

"Do you think someone is trying to sabotage our trip?"

"Something's going on," Charlee said, finishing her business. She stood, zipping her pants back up. She looked down to check that her stream didn't hit her pants.

Nothing.

That was one of things that she missed about civilization. Toilets. Satisfied, she stood up straight to leave and saw a human figure standing a few yards away.

She let loose a scream, backing up quickly toward Malena. The figure was tall and bulky. In the shadows, the only thing she could tell was that it must be a man.

"What—" Malena's eyes widened as she gasped. Charlee ran toward her friend, not looking back, her supplies forgotten as they both took off running toward the campground.

Charlee's heart pounded in her chest as she ran. Luckily, still wearing her boots, she was able to get a good grip in the dirt and mud as she ran. Two figures ran toward them as they broke through the trees.

West and Luka.

"What is it?" he demanded, grabbing her by her shoulders.

"A man," she gasped, pointing in the direction from which they had just come from.

"Stay with the others," he shouted before taking off into the trees, Luka right behind him.

"Everything okay?" Dr. Zhang rushed toward them, concern on his face.

"Someone's in the woods," Malena began to explain as they walked to the center of their camp.

Charlee darted off toward her tent. West and Luka had run off into the woods without any weapons. If it was a poacher, they would almost surely have a gun on them.

She dove in and rustled for her backpack. Her hand met the cool hard steel handle of her small handgun. She dug farther, looking for her flashlight. She exited the tent, brandishing her handgun and flashlight. She took the safety off and jogged back toward the trees.

"Charlee!" Malena shouted. "He said for us to stay with the others."

She ignored her friend as she entered back into the woods, this time armed. She wanted to kick herself for not taking her gun with her the first time. They had just had a powwow about safety, and her and Malena went straight into the woods unarmed. This time she was ready, and whoever was in the woods had better watch out.

Charlee tried to slow her breathing down as she slowly crept through the dense forest. She kept the gun aimed in front of her with her flashlight providing a small line of light. She could hear voices off in the distance. Not sure if it was West and Luka, she kept her weapon trained in front of her. She pushed down her nerves and blew out a deep breath. She tried to imagine that this was a hunting trip, like the ones she would take with her family. It was almost the same. She was in search of her target.

Hunting.

Charlee had done it plenty of times and knew to keep her wits about her and her aim steady. Her father's voice echoed in her head, as if he were walking with her.

Hold steady.

She came to an area where the trees thinned out. She stepped out of the brush, the moonlight providing extra light. She looked around and lowered her gun.

"West," she breathed, relaxing as he spun around.

"I thought I told you to stay with the others," he snapped. There was a wild look in his eyes that she had never seen before.

Something wasn't right. She looked around and saw no signs of Luka.

"Where's Luka?" she asked, her heart rate increasing as she waited for his answer. Her grip tightened on the handle of the weapon. It provided a slight comfort, but she needed West to answer her question.

"Go back to the camp," he urged as he slowly stepped to her.

"I came to help." Her nerves began to build as he didn't answer her questions. "You guys took off so fast, and without any weapons. Poachers carry guns."

"Charlee, please, just—"

Her eyes darted behind him as the brush to his right parted and out stepped a massive tiger.

"West, watch out!" she screamed, taking aim. His head snapped around toward the tiger and back to her.

"Charlee, no!" West yelled, dashing in front of the tiger.

Her finger paused on the trigger as confusion set in. Why would West be dashing in front of a wild tiger? And why wasn't the tiger attacking him?

What in the hell was going on?

She froze in place, unsure of what to do. Her mouth dropped open as the tiger came and stood beside West. She slowly lowered her gun, but refused to take her finger off the trigger.

"What is going on?" she whispered, stepping back, unable to look away from the tiger.

"Charlee!" West called her name sharply, gaining her attention. She glanced back at him as he slowly approached her with his hands in the air. "Baby, look at me. There are some things we need to talk about. This wasn't how I wanted to tell you."

"Tell me what?" she asked, shaking her head. "Why is that tiger not attacking us? It's just standing there like it knows you."

"Because he does," West admitted. She gasped, and her eyes wandered back to the tiger who just stood there and stared at them.

"Stop moving," she warned, her voice growing stronger. She raised her gun and pointed it at West. "I mean it. Stay back."

"You're not going to shoot me," West pointed out, taking another step toward her. "Do you trust me?"

"Tell me what's going on," she pleaded. "Stop moving!"

He came forward and pressed his chest to the barrel of her gun, gently covering her hand with his.

"Put the gun down, Charlee," he demanded. She stared into his eyes and was torn. Her heart softened. His eyes told it all. He wouldn't hurt her.

She lowered the gun.

He released a deep breath and crushed her to him, his large hands gripping the back of her neck.

"I wish we had more time," he murmured in her ear.

"What's going on? You're scaring me." She pulled away from him and looked at the tiger.

"I was going to tell you, but I guess there's no time like the present." He sighed as he backed up from her. He began to strip his clothes off.

"What the hell are you doing?" she cried out, confusion mounting as she watched him remove his underwear before falling to all fours on the ground. Her eyes grew wide as she watched fur burst forth on his skin. His body drew longer and transitioned into that of a tiger.

If she hadn't see it with her own eyes, she would have sworn that she was crazy.

Maybe she was.

Maybe this was a dream and she was in a coma somewhere. She must have fell back there when she ran from the dark figure.

She shook her head in disbelief and began backing up, away from West, or what she thought was West. She paused as the scientist in her pushed forth.

How was this possible?

She slowly walked forward, toward West. Her heart slammed against her chest as she stood in front of the beautiful animal. Its intelligent eyes stared back at her. Her free hand reached up slowly, itching to touch the massive head. As if sensing her hesitation, the animal turned its head and pushed it into her hand.

Charlee gasped at the feel of the tiger's dense fur beneath her fingers. Its chest rumbled as she ran her fingers across it's head and gave a little scratch behind its ears. She chuckled as it pushed against her hand again. It was like a house cat who loved having its ears scratched and head rubbed.

"West?" she whispered his name. The cat looked at her, then it really hit her. Her lover had just transformed into a massive tiger. "Is it really you?"

The tiger released a chuff as it nodded its head.

"How is this possible?" she asked in disbelief, using both of her hands to rub his head.

"We were born this way." Luka's voice appeared from behind her.

Her head snapped in the direction of his voice, finding him emerging from the trees. She took note that he said we.

"This is…how do you…I mean…" she couldn't formulate a single question. Her mind was racing with every question she could possibly think of as West walked away.

"He got away," Luka announced to the tigers.

"Go ahead and go back. Charlee and I need to talk." West's voice appeared from behind her. She turned and found his naked human form standing close to her. She watched the tiger hop back into the brush, and Luka disappeared into the trees.

Her eyes turned back to West and she swallowed hard. His eyes searched for something in hers. She didn't even know where to start, so she just waited.

NINETEEN

West stared down at Charlee. Her wide eyes gave way to her confusion and fear. Hell, he didn't blame her. This was not the way he had planned to tell her about his tiger. He just didn't have a choice. He'd seen her in action with a gun and knew that her aim was perfect. He couldn't risk her shooting Drago. The bullet wouldn't have killed him, but he would have been one pissed off security specialist. West would have had to pay his friend a heavy tip for the taking of a bullet.

"We need to talk," he breathed, running his fingers through his hair. Charlee jerked her head in a nod. He grabbed his clothes and began to dress. He wasn't sure how to begin, but he figured he would just start from the beginning. "I was born this way."

"That's not possible," she whispered, shaking her head.

"Well, I hate to break it to you, Doctor, but it is."

"But how have we not known? Scientists would—"

"Would have studied my people under a microscope. Humans have a funny way of trying to eradicate something they don't understand. It's best that humans don't know about shifters." He shook his head sadly. His parents had drilled it into his head as a kid that humans could never know. Every shifter knew the dangers of what could happen if the humans found out that they were not the only ones inhabiting the Earth. It would lead to pure chaos.

"So what? Shifters just hide from everyone?" she asked.

"No. There are all types of shifters, and they live everyday lives, just like humans. They attend college, have careers, settle down and have families. There's only one difference between a human and a shifter." He stepped toward her slowly. His tiger was pleased that she didn't flinch as he reached for her. He needed to touch her. He knew that he and his tiger would not be able to handle it if she shunned them.

"So, do humans and shifters get married?" she asked as his fingers gently brushed her hair from her face. He tucked the strands behind her ear and nodded.

"And procreate too." Her eyes widened, and he could see her mind running wild.

"And the children?"

"More than likely, they will be shifters. About ninety-eight percent of children born to mixed races will inherit the shifter gene. It tends to be the dominant one." He chuckled at the array of facial expressions that swept across her face.

"So that's why this sanctuary means so much to you," she acknowledged, grabbing hold of his hand, entwining their fingers together. She stepped closer to him, tilting her head back.

"Yes, this place means everything to me. We have to prevent tigers from becoming extinct." His eyes gazed off in the distance. His heart clenched with the thought of losing the Amur tigers, or any tigers for that matter.

"Can real tigers tell the difference from shifters?"

He barked out a laugh and drew her close in a hug. Confusion lined her face as she pulled back.

"What did I say?"

"Real tigers? I promise you, my dear, that my tiger is real." He feigned hurt, holding his chest. His tiger stood at attention and pushed at his chest. It demanded to be free again, just to prove to her that he was certainly real.

"Oh," she breathed, lowering her eyes in embarrassment. "I didn't mean any disrespect."

"None taken. My tiger is wanting to get out again to prove to you that he's most certainly real," West said. He pushed his tiger back in an attempt to calm it down. It whined, but settled down.

"You can speak to it?"

"We're one in the same. When I'm in my human form, he's just in the background. Sometimes he likes to let the alpha in him come to the surface, but I'm always in control. Even when I'm in my animal form, I'm right there with him," he explained to her.

"I won't tell anyone," she promised. "I mean it. What you said about scientists is right. They would ruin everything that your people have worked so hard to accomplish. It would literally be a circus."

"Thank you," he replied.

They drew quiet, and he didn't know what else to say. He didn't want to rush any decisions from her, but he just had to know.

Would she accept him as he was?

"I guess we better get back to the camp," she stated, squeezing his hand with hers. He glanced down at their entwined fingers and felt a little spark of hope for them.

"Yes, I'm sure they're probably worried with you jetting off into the woods, guns blazing," he noted with a dry chuckle. They began making their way back to the campground.

"What?" she scoffed. "I thought I was coming to rescue you, but here you are, a big bad tiger."

"But seriously, you shouldn't have come back into the woods," he warned, pulling to a stop. He turned her to him, needing her to look at him. He didn't know what he would do should something happen to her. "Promise me, next time I give you an order to stay put, you will."

"Hopefully, there won't be a next time," she joked, but he didn't crack a smile. He was serious. His animal grumbled with the thought of her not listening and something happening to her.

"I mean it. I don't want you in any danger. I can handle it. Promise me, Charlee," he pleaded.

He had never begged for anything in his life before. As one of the wealthiest tiger families, he had everything in the world that he could ask for, but for her safety, he would. Just in the short time he had gotten to know her, she had found a way into his heart.

He needed her.

He would do whatever he must to protect her.

"Okay," she whispered, staring up at him with her large eyes.

Satisfied, they continued onward to the camp.

"Charlee!" Malena exclaimed, running over and snatching Charlee up into a bear hug. "Are you all right?"

"Yes, I'm fine," Charlee assured her as they began to talk softly amongst each other.

West's eyes met Luka's as he came forward with the rest of the group.

"I was just telling everyone how the guy got away," Luka informed him. West was confident that Luka didn't tell them any more information than was needed.

"This just goes to show that we need to take this seriously," West announced. "We're in the middle of nowhere, and the only way we can keep each other safe is to have one another's backs. Let's get a good night's rest, and remember to partner up."

The groups began to disperse, and West wasn't sure if Charlee was going to come with him or go back to her tent that she had shared with Malena originally. His tiger let out a whine as he turned to walk toward his tent. It tried to get him to change direction and walk back to Charlee.

It'll be all right, he murmured to his tiger. He didn't know who he was trying to convince, him or the tiger.

"West! Wait for me," Charlee called out.

He turned to find her jogging to him as Malena headed to her tent. His heart sped up as he watched Charlee get closer to him. This was it. She would break off what they had and be done with him. He barked out a laugh in his head at the thought.

The infamous West Rogavac had fallen for a woman.

He knew the guys would ride him hard if he ever mentioned the thoughts and doubts that raced through his mind.

"Hey," she murmured as she stopped in front of him, leaving just the two of them in the middle of the campground. The nervous look in her eyes had his heart speeding up. He braced himself as he waited for her to speak. "I meant to ask you, can you show me what it means to be a tiger in bed?"

Charlee's breaths came fast and hard as she settled her sweaty body against West's. Her body tingled in the afterglow of their lovemaking.

West was definitely a tiger in bed.

A whimsical smile lingered on her lips as she thought back to his facial expression when she had ran over to him. His shoulders had drooped slightly when he turned to walk back to his tent. Her heart swelled with his disappointment that he tried to hide.

But she saw it.

She had come to terms with him being a tiger shifter before they had made it back to the camp. She could literally feel the nervous vibes pouring off him as they made the journey back to join the others. She considered herself a modern scientist and knew that it would be ignorant of her to assume that they were the only ones walking the Earth.

She had quickly gotten to know West and knew that he was an honorable man. So what? His body could transform into one of the most powerful animals on the planet. The memories of his cat pushing its massive head against her still had her in awe.

Her body shuddered as West's finger burned a trail down the center of her spine. He pushed her hair off her moist forehead with the other hand as he turned to look at her. He leaned down and covered her mouth with his in a deep, passionate kiss.

A deep moan escaped her as she reached up and threaded her fingers in his hair. She wished that they could stay in their little secluded tent forever. Nothing to interrupt them, just the two of them alone, in a tent under the stars.

He pulled back and placed a chaste kiss to her lips. Complete darkness surrounded them.

"Can you see in the dark?" she whispered, straining to see his facial expression.

"Pretty much," he chuckled. He shifted, tucking her in the crook of his arm. She held back a moan, loving the feel of his muscular form against her softer body. Her hand settled on his chest as she stared off into the darkness.

"What made you decide to come to me?" His voice broke the silence.

She tilted her head back, unable to see his eyes. But she could feel them on her as she contemplated why she didn't take off for the hills screaming.

"Seeing your tiger, I just had this feeling that he wouldn't hurt me. That he would keep me safe, no matter what. I don't know how to explain it—"

"He would never harm you." West cut her off as his arm squeezed her, bringing her flush against him. Her breath caught in her throat as she felt her core clench. She groaned internally. What was it about West that kept her body coiled, ready for him?

Sheer animal magnetism?

She giggled at the thought.

"What's so funny?" he murmured, placing a kiss on the top of her head.

"I just don't understand how my body is just so drawn to you," she murmured, trailing a finger down his chest. "It's like there's a low electric current beneath my skin, and the minute you touch me, it hits me full force."

"Same here," he replied, threading his fingers in her hair to pull her head back. Her breaths came quicker and her thighs clenched together in anticipation. She could feel the slickness coat her thighs as she waited. "But it will have to be later. You need sleep. Everyone will be waking in about an hour."

He released her hair and she blew out a deep breath. How the hell was she supposed to sleep now?

TWENTY

West glanced back at the group to make sure everyone was accounted for. Today would be the last leg of their extended stay in the wild. They would be returning back to the main sanctuary. They were running low on supplies, and it was time for Charlee and the biologists to touch base with the ecologists and senior researchers. According to the group, there was plenty of information that needed to be discussed.

Today, they would try for one more tiger, then they would head back. After the scare yesterday with the man in the woods, and Alf's records going missing, the entire group knew not to separate. Each member wore their weapons on them somewhere they could access them easily if need be. There was no telling if they would run across a wild animal or a mysterious human.

They didn't need to go far from the trucks this time. There were a few direct paths that they could walk that led away from where they parked the trucks. They were following the multiple sets of tracks of different animals.

His tiger was currently pleased that Charlee chose them. His animal was calmer and satisfied. Hell, West was satisfied with the urgency of their lovemaking from this morning. He wanted to shout to the world for all to hear when he climaxed, but knew that because they were in such open accommodations, he had to remain as quiet as a mouse in church. He couldn't wait to get Charlee back to the States. He planned to lock her up in his bedroom for two whole weeks. She would scream his name until she no longer had a voice. His pants drew stiff with all of the thoughts that burned in his mind. He glanced back and found her eyes on him. She smiled slightly as she gripped her shotgun in her hand.

He drew his attention back to the mission at hand—finding another tiger to insert the microchip into. West paused and bent down to study the ground. Familiar tracks were embedded in the dry mud.

Tiger tracks.

"We're going in the right direction," he announced, standing up. "There are a few different tracks that I can see. It looks like wild boars have passed this way. A hungry tiger is probably following them."

Everyone nodded as they prepared. West's eyes caught Luka's and he knew that something was wrong. Luka casually signaled for them to go on, but he was staying behind. West nodded and motioned for everyone to continue.

The forest began to thin out and West held up a hand, signaling for everyone to pause. He moved forward and parted the dense brush so that he could see. He was surprised to find that the area opened to a few acres of flat land that was full of elk mulling around. Off in the distance, West's eyes caught sight of a tiger keeping his body low to the ground as he slowly approached the elk herd.

The tiger was in complete hunter's mode. West knew that feeling all too well. His tiger loved the thrill of the hunt. He had to push down his tiger who wanted to join in. West quickly closed the brush and turned back to the group.

"We have a tiger on the hunt. There's a herd of elk out there," he said.

"Elk? Really?" Charlee said, moving up from the middle of the group. "We either do this now and risk setting off an elk stampede, or we wait until he makes his kill, then we get him."

"We are not going to have time," Dr. Skobo announced. "We might as well wait and let the cat eat first before we knock him out."

"But if we wait until after the kill, we run the risk of scavengers coming and interrupting us as we tag him. That could prevent us from getting the information that we need," Dr. Zhang advised the group.

"Dr. Zhang is right." West nodded. "If we wait until after, we'll need to at least wait until he moves away from the carcass so that scavengers can just have the rest and leave us be."

A loud commotion filled the air, letting them know that the decision was out of their hands. West flew back to the brush and moved the leaves, watching as the tiger moved. Everyone rushed over so that they could watch nature in action. The slight sounds of cameras clicking filled the air as everyone was captivated by the sight of the tiger weeding out his prey.

Not a word was said as they all watched the tiger run along with the elk. West knew that the tiger was testing the herd and trying to determine the young, weak, and older elks.

Quickly, the tiger identified his prey. A larger elk, who was slower than the others, somehow separated from the herd. The group of elks continued on as the lone elk seemed dazed and confused that it was alone. The tiger instantly sped up with his body angled, and headed straight for its target. Its powerful strides ate up the distance. In what seemed to move in slow motion, but actually spanned a few seconds, the tiger pounced on the elk's back.

The elk released a cry as it fell to the ground. Its legs kicked out as the tiger dodged them, and flew to the elk's neck. It latched onto its throat and they all waited as they watched nature play out.

"Wow," Charlee breathed from beside West. Murmurs of agreement floated through the air. "Too bad for the elk, but that was just beautiful."

"I second that," Malena agreed as she adjusted her backpack.

Luka slowly crept back into the group. None of them had even realized he had been missing. The look in his eyes let West know that he found something. West itched to pull him aside to find out what was going on, but knew that would alert the humans.

West and Luka stood guard while they all worked on the tiger. So far, this was the biggest tiger they had captured. Silence filled the air as each person did the job that they were assigned. This time, they didn't have time.

Charlee was able to shoot the tiger with the tranquilizer as it was jogging back to the brush, but it was still a couple hundred feet from its kill. It had been an easy shot. The tiger's belly was full from its meal. The scavengers would be coming soon, and they did not want to be caught by a sleeping tiger. The hyenas and buzzards would not be friendly, and chances were high that the hyenas would attack.

Charlee quickly examined the tiger's teeth and mouth, finding them to be in perfect shape. It's massive fangs displayed how dangerous it would be if it woke up with them still working on it. This was an impressive male Amur tiger. His body was in shape, and there were no signs of physical injuries to him. It was absolutely breathtaking, but Charlee did not have the time to admire him.

"You need to hurry," West advised with his back to them. They both held weapons in their hands so they wouldn't be taken by surprise by any of the wild animals in the area.

"I can't get the chip to register," Alf stated, frustration lining his voice.

"What's the screen saying?" Luka asked, turning his head toward them. Alf blew out a deep breath as he tapped the screen. Luka gave him verbal instructions to help him get the chip registered.

Charlee scrambled as she wrote down her measurements. She began packing up her supplies as her ears picked up on West letting loose a string of curses. Her head whipped around to see the first hyena making its way toward the dead elk.

"It's time to go," West snapped to the group, just as Alf confirmed that the chip was showing on the tablet.

Everyone scrambled to grab their bags as Luka and West began stalking toward them. Charlee's eyes widened as two more hyenas came out of the brush on the other side of the clearing.

"What are we going to do about the tiger?" Charlee asked as she stood. They couldn't just leave the tiger alone while the hyenas were with the carcass. The hyenas would see it as another opportunity for a meal on an unconscious tiger.

"You all go hide in the brush. Luka and I will handle the hyenas," he instructed, motioning for them to get moving. Charlee peeked around him and could see that the hyenas were taking notice of them as they attacked the fresh carcass. More of the hyenas appeared, going straight for the carcass.

She glanced back down at the slumbering tiger, knowing that it would be out for at least another twenty minutes or so before it would start coming out of its drug-induced sleep. There was no way that they would be able to move seven hundred pounds of dead weight. It would take all of them, and looking over at the carcass, they didn't have much time.

West glanced back and cursed. "Get moving now!" he snapped. The group began to jog toward the trees. Charlee turned, but saw that West and Luka hadn't budged from their spots near the tiger.

"Aren't you guys coming?" she asked, pushing her hair from her face.

"We can't leave him unprotected. Go with the others. We'll be fine," West assured her as he came to stand in front of her.

"Looks like their whole pack is now at the elk's body," Luka announced over his shoulder.

"It'll be fine. The hyenas won't attack when they see that there are other tigers in the neighborhood," he murmured against her temple. "Take everyone a little deeper into the woods. Just go about a few hundred feet and wait for us."

"Are you going to shift?" she asked. She wanted to see his tiger again.

"No, but they'll know that our animals are close." He turned and pushed her toward the brush where Malena and the others waited. She jogged to the brush, clueless as to what West and Luka had planned.

"Come on, " she instructed as she motioned for everyone to follow her. "West said for us to move back in the brush. They'll come as soon as the tiger looks as if it's waking."

"What is so special about them that the hyena's will not attack?" Dr. Skobo snapped.

"I don't know." She threw her hands in the air. "Maybe the guns that they have in their hands."

"Let's just do as Mr. Rogavac asked," Alf encouraged. "He hasn't led us wrong yet."

They stuck together as they made it a little deeper into the forest before finding a good place to rest. Charlee couldn't concentrate on the conversations that were softly going on around her as her imagination began to race. What was West and Luka doing in order to keep the scavengers away from the tiger? Would they be okay? Would they have to shift and defend the large unconscious tiger?

Charlee sighed as she leaned back against the tree she had sat down in front of. It shouldn't take the tiger that much longer before it would begin to awaken. She glanced down at her watch and saw that not that much time had passed.

"It's very brave of them to stay and guard the tiger," Malena said as she sat next to Charlee.

Charlee ached to tell her friend West and Luka's secret, but knew that it was not her place to divulge that information. Her and Malena had been best friends for so long, and this would be the first true secret that she would have to withhold from her friend.

"That they are," she murmured.

TWENTY ONE

West and Luka made their way back to the brush. The tiger had finally begun to stir. While waiting on the tiger to wake, they both pushed their alpha powers out. When doing this, their tigers were right beneath the surface. A step away from shifting, but it would let any enemy know that the powerful animal was close. It always confused animals so they tended to slink away, unsure of where the animals were. The hyenas stayed near the elk, choosing to ignore them instead.

"Drago captured one of the humans that had been tracking us," Luka informed West as they entered back into the forest.

"Where are they?" West asked, pausing. This was a step in the right direction. They had known someone was following them from the moment they had left the trucks to travel by foot.

"They're located near the vehicles. He'll wait to hear from you," Luka stated.

West grew excited at the thought of finally making headway in finding out who was doing the poaching and targeting the group. He knew that Drago was a specialist at getting information from the man. No matter if the guy refused to talk, Drago always had a way.

"I'll call him on the satellite phone once we get back to the trucks."

West stopped dead in his tracks as his ears picked up on something.

Silence.

No birds chirping, no mating calls. Nothing. The forest had drawn silent, causing his tiger to instantly take notice. Silence was never a good thing in the wild.

West's eyes flew to Luka's, and West knew that he recognized the silence too. They both took off running in the direction that the team had disappeared. His heart pounded in his chest as he

raced forward. The silence was shattered by the single sound of gunfire, followed by another one. The repeated sounds filled the air.

An automatic weapon.

"Get to the scientists!" West yelled. Luka disappeared deeper into the trees.

West crashed through the brush toward the direction that the gunfire was coming from. His tiger slammed into his chest, begging to be let free.

Not yet.

West wanted to see who it was that would dare open fire on peaceful scientists. West's shifter hearing picked up on muttered Russian curses. He pushed harder and finally broke through the brush, coming upon the man as he bent down to reload his weapon.

Fury burned in West's chest as he leapt forward. Surprise crossed the gunman's face as West swung his fist, packed full of his shifter strength. His knuckles burned as his fist connected with the man's jaw.

The gunman's face snapped back as he fell to the ground. West stood over the still man, breathing hard as he tried to control his tiger. His animal, enraged, clawed at his chest, not taking no for an answer. West bent over in agony as he tried to push his animal back. He gasped in pain, having never before lost control of his tiger.

The internal battle of wills was overwhelming, but it was West who won the battle. His tiger snarled as it paced beneath his skin. West straightened back to his full height, taking deep breaths before leaning over to check for a pulse on the man.

Nothing.

Blood poured out of the dead man's mouth and onto the ground beneath him. His jaw remained open at an odd angle, unhinged. West knew that his shifter power was behind the force that killed the man with one blow. He flexed his hand, ignoring the stinging of the broken skin on his knuckles.

The animal in him was somewhat satisfied by the death. He would have preferred to play out the death a little longer, if only to gain information. West went through the dead man's pockets, looking for any form of identification. He grabbed the duffle bag that lied next to him and found a Russian driver's license.

Pitosin B. Semyonovich.

Who the hell was this guy? West glanced back at the still figure, pocketing the identification card in his pocket before turning back to the bag.

West continued to go through it and found it full of ammunition for the automatic rifle. A Russian newspaper article was folded in the bag, stuffed inside an inner pocket. West unfolded the paper and found a black and white photo of one Dr. Charlee Black. The article discussed her team's trip from the United States to Russia, and the purpose of the month-long study. He pocketed the article as well.

West's tiger let loose a deep growl with the thought that one of the scientists could be injured, or better yet, Charlee—

Charlee!

Fear crept into his chest as he took off, leaving the dead man for the scavengers to find. His tiger roared as he frantically pushed his body hard, trying to get to her. He heard shouting not too far ahead and he pushed even harder. His tiger lent his speed, allowing West to move faster. He ignored the slapping of branches and leaves against his body as he flew threw the forest.

The voices grew louder as he burst through the dense brush and onto the beaten path where the group had been waiting before they were attacked. Everyone looked to be frantic and scared, but unharmed. West, breathing hard, turned in search of Charlee.

His tiger slammed into his chest at the sight of Charlee on the ground, leaning back against a tree with Luka pressing a blood-soaked rag to her arm. His tiger wanted to rush back to the dead gunman and rip him to shreds for harming Charlee. But instead, he rushed to her side, falling to his knees. Malena's sobs filled the air as she turned away, walking over to the others.

"Charlee," he murmured. His hand shook slightly as he gently pushed her hair away from her pale face. Her pain-filled eyes opened and turned to him.

"West. You're okay," she sighed, a small smile gracing her lips. Her eyes closed again as pain racked her body. West shot Luka a hard look. Luka nodded his understanding of West's message.

Be careful.

"I'm here." He motioned for Luka to remove the cloth so that they could see the wound.

"It went clean through," Luka murmured, leaning close to examine Charlee's arm.

"What happened to the shooter?" she asked, grimacing as she shifted.

"He's been taken care of," West said, keeping his voice low where she and Luka were the only ones to hear. Her eyes snapped open at his announcement.

"Is that why your hand is bruised and bloodied?" she whispered.

"Don't worry about me," he said, ignoring her observation. His hand would heal soon due to his shifter genes. In about an hour, it would be just a light bruising, and by nightfall, there would be no evidence that his fist had killed a human.

"Hold this so I can get the first-aid kit out of my bag," Luka barked out, switching positions with West.

West hated causing her any bit of pain, but they had to stop the bleeding. One centimeter to the left and the bullet would have hit her brachial artery. Hitting an artery would have meant more blood and she would have bled to death before getting her back to the main sanctuary.

"Here, this has a bio agent that will help plug the hole," Luka said, turning back to them.

West moved out the way to allow his friend to work. Creating wonders that could save people's lives was Luka's specialty. West knew that this agent was something that Luka had just got approval for, for use in the field in the armed forces.

"Luka will fix you up good," West murmured, grabbing her hand. She squeezed hard as Luka began to clean the area. West glanced around and nodded to the other team members. Everyone was accounted for. Shook up, but otherwise alive and unharmed.

"Did you get anything out of him before you took care of him?" Luka asked in a low voice.

"No, but I got his identification card in my pocket. There was nothing but ammo in his bag."

"So this was planned," Luka stipulated.

"But why?" she hissed as he began wrapping gauze around her bicep.

"I think they're after you," West admitted.

"Me? But why?" she cried out. West motioned for her to keep her voice down. He didn't want to attract the others. He didn't want anyone to know his theory yet. Hell, he was still trying to piece it together himself.

Poachers wanted tiger's pelts and bones. A famous biologist and her team coming to help save the animals by fighting for stricter laws to protect the animals would mean that the poachers would lose a lot of money.

Tons.

Enough that they would be willing to kill for it. West refused to let that happen. Charlee meant too much to him. She had crawled in and took up space in his heart, and right now, he didn't want her to leave. He didn't even want to know what his future would be without her.

"Don't worry about it now," he murmured, running a finger down her face. He couldn't resist touching her. His tiger, now calmed, still didn't like the fact that she was injured. He wanted to nuzzle her and rub up against her, just to check her out for himself, but West pushed him back.

Not today, but soon, he promised his animal.

"Okay, I think that should hold. We should drive straight to the sanctuary so that we can have someone else take a look," Luka suggested.

"Thank you, Luka," she whispered, tears flowing down her cheeks. West tried to wipe them away, but they continued to flow.

"You're welcome. Last thing, let's make you a sling so that we can keep that arm up."

West and Luka made a makeshift sling to keep her arm elevated and close to her body. West helped her stand, bringing her body against his so that she could get her bearings.

"Dizzy?" he asked. She nodded as she leaned into him.

"Here," Malena offered, pulling a water bottle out of her backpack. He took the bottle and helped Charlee take a few sips before handing it back to Malena. Charlee swayed a little as she tried to stand on her own. He bent down and scooped her up into his arms and turned to the group.

"Okay, everyone. Let's make it back to the trucks. Eyes open, guns out. We're all accounted for, so shoot first and ask questions later."

TWENTY TWO

"Take two of these pain pills and rest tonight," Dr. Kargina Romanova instructed Charlee. West leaned back against the wall of his suite at the sanctuary. He didn't want her anywhere else but his quarters. One of the benefits of the family donating millions of dollars was a private suite on the property in the housing building for the employees of the sanctuary.

Due to Charlee's injury, they chose to take her back to the main building of the sanctuary. Before arriving, they had made a pit stop at the base camp so that everyone could go there as originally planned, but since Charlee was shot, West, Luka, and Malena brought her back to the main building for medical attention.

They had driven nonstop, calling in ahead that they had an injured person. The local medical team had met them outside once they drove up to the building. Dr. Romanova was the Russian concierge physician on staff at the sanctuary.

A knock at the door broke through West's thoughts. He walked over to the door and opened it slightly. He relaxed at the sight of a refreshed Malena standing at the door.

"How is she?" she asked, walking through the door.

"She's doing fine," Charlee mumbled, trying to sit up in bed on her one good arm before flopping back against the plush pillows.

"Now take it easy," Dr. Romanova gently scolded. "Here, let me help you."

West walked to the foot of the bed as the doctor and Malena helped Charlee get more comfortable. Both he and his tiger felt helpless as they watched Charlee wrestle with her pain. He would have taken the bullet for her without a second thought, just to spare her the pain.

"Take it easy tonight and get some rest," the doctor instructed as she gathered her medical bag. "Don't let her out of this bed unless she needs to use the restroom, then straight back."

"Don't worry about it, Doctor, we'll make sure she rests," Malena said as she helped Charlee sip a glass of water to take the pain pills.

"You couldn't pay me to get out of this bed." Charlee yawned and slid farther beneath the covers. "I have truly missed the comforts of a real bed after spending so much time in the wild and sleeping on the ground in tents.

"Mr. Rogavac, can I ask you a question?" The doctor switched over to Russian and motioned for West to follow her to the door. He took one last glance at Charlee to see her and Malena speaking quietly.

"Is there something I can do for you, Doctor?" he asked as he followed her into the hallway. He shut the door quietly behind him.

"The materials that I found in her wound is something that I have never seen before. Where did it come from?" Her eyes were wide in anticipation. He held in his chuckle at the excitement on her face. "It cauterized the small vessels to completely stop the bleeding, and it looks as if it has an enzyme in it—"

He held up his hand and shook his head. "You're going to have to speak to my lead biomedical engineer, Luka Batalo. He designed it in our labs."

"I would love to speak with him," she said, reaching into her bag. She handed him her business card. "Please, have him call me. I have so many questions."

"I'll pass it on to him." West nodded.

"Please do, and call me anytime for Dr. Black if she needs anything."

"Will do," he said with a nod as the physician walked off. His phone buzzed in his pocket. Pulling it out, he looked down at the glass screen and saw Luka's name appear. He slid his finger against the smooth screen. "Yeah."

"Hey, I just spoke with Drago and updated him on what happened. He wants to meet with us. He got the information we needed out of the human."

"Where?" West slowly twisted the handle to this suite and opened the door slightly so that he could check on Charlee. Malena had crawled into the bed with her, and they both were dozing off.

"Over in Kutsk at the Tiger Eye Tavern."

"Fine. I'll be down in five." West pressed the end button and crept into the room. He didn't want to disturb Charlee, but he couldn't resist checking on her.

The tavern that Drago wanted to meet at was owned by a local tiger shifter that West knew. Kutsk was the next town over, and the tavern would be a safe place to meet and discuss sensitive information.

He walked over to her side of the bed and found her asleep. He bent down and placed a gentle kiss on her forehead. He glanced over and found Malena staring at him.

"She's head over heels for you, you know," Malena said softly.

"And I for her," he replied.

"Don't hurt her." She yawned and snuggled down farther into the bed and closed her eyes.

"Never. This I promise."

"Drago," West greeted his friend with an outstretched hand. The security specialist gripped his hand in a firm shake as they sat down at the small table located in the back of the tavern. They would have plenty of privacy. Drago's men, Ivan and Gerald, stood watch with their backs to the table. No one would dare interrupt.

Drago raised a finger, summoning the waitress. The woman looked to be in her mid-thirties. She had dirty blonde hair pulled up in a high ponytail, with jeans and a black T-shirt with the tavern's logo splashed across the front.

"What can I get you?" she asked, quickly taking their orders. She didn't appear to be intimidated at all by the large guards standing around them. West knew that this establishment drew in shifters of all kinds.

"I hear that there was some action after we left," Drago stated.

West went into detail on the shooting, but paused as the waitress returned with their drinks. She quickly handed them out and promised to return soon to check in on them.

"The fucker shot Charlee," West growled, trying to tame his feline. He reached into his pocket and pulled out the identification card and the newspaper clipping before placing them on the table.

Drago dragged them across and studied them.

"This definitely confirms that they're after her," Drago murmured.

"Yes, but I need to know who the hell they are," West snapped, taking a drink of his straight vodka. The cool liquid burned slightly as it slid down his throat. He was not worried about drinking too much tonight. With his shifter metabolism, he would burn off the alcohol before they even left the bar.

"The human we captured sung me a very pretty song," Drago drawled, his eyes intense.

"Talk,"West demanded. This was the closest they had been to finding out who was orchestrating the attacks.

"Vitya Nikitovich was hired to follow the good doctor and sabotage her expedition. This assignment was for him to become a Vor." Drago took a sip of his drink.

"A made man,"West murmured. His tiger began to pace beneath his skin as he waited for Drago to continue. West grew up in a Russian family that still had ties to the homeland. He certainly knew of a few Russian Mafia pakhans, or bosses.

"And you'll never guess which Bratva he was trying to be made in to." West already knew that he wouldn't like the answer. Every brushing he had with the Bratva's, or brotherhoods of Russia, left him feeling dirty.

"Which one?" Luka asked.

"The Ruslanovich Bratva," Drago informed the table. West's paused, drink to his lips, at the words of his security specialist.

"Is that so?" West murmured, taking a sip from his glass. He didn't taste any of the liquid as Drago continued.

"According to the human, the Ruslanovich Bratva was working with the top Chinese poachers. They had a trade deal between the Russian Mafia and the Chinese Triad. This deal is worth millions, and the poaching side of their industry is being threatened by your woman, Dr. Black."

West grew still as his mind flew with the worst-case scenario, and he knew without asking that it was probably about to play out. He knew the leader of the Ruslanovich Bratva, better than he would like to.

"What else?" West questioned. He knew there would be more. He gripped his glass tight as he waited for Drago to answer.

"The Bratva put out a contract on Dr. Charlee Black."

The sound of glass shattering filled the air at the admission. West glanced down and found that he had crushed the glass in his hand. He shook off the small shards as his tiger let loose a growl.

The waitress, hearing the glass shatter, rushed over with extra napkins and wiped the table clean. He slowly wiped his hands with the napkins, ensuring that there was no glass embedded in his palm. The waitress hurried away, promising to bring another round of drinks for them.

Charlee was a brilliant species specialist, and she was making a hell of a difference in the world for endangered animals. Her lectures and speaking engagements took her all around the world. She focused not only on the animals themselves, but shed light on the black market and was getting more countries to side with her and ban poaching.

Because of her lifelong work, countries with high poaching rates were cracking down on the black market business. If the Bratva was able to take her out, it would be a while before someone else would gain enough momentum to make a difference. Without Charlee, everything could slowly go back to the way it was before she had taken the world by storm.

The Ruslanovich Bratva was run by Tabakov Danilovich, grandson to the founder, Solomin Ruslanovich. Tabakov was a businessman with corrupt dealings all over the world, some even in the United States. West tried to avoid him over the years. He didn't want his family's name and business associated with the crooked businessman.

The Ruslanovich and the Rogavac's, unfortunately, shared a history, one that dated back to the era of West and Tabakov's grandfathers, Galdin Rogavac and Solomin Ruslanovich, in the days of Joseph Stalin. During the reign of Stalin, both Galdin and Solomin were small-time criminals and were thrust into the gulags, Soviet labor camps.

There was a fight for power amongst groups in the gulags, where a war of sorts broke out. It was Galdin who had saved Solomin's life while they were in the labor camp. As a thank you for saving his life, Solomin promised that whenever a Rogavac called on the Ruslanovich family, any request would be honored. Over the years, the Rogavacs had never had any need to ask of anything from the Ruslanovich family.

West knew what he would have to do. He would have to pay a visit to the Russian pakhan. He sat back in his chair, dreading the meeting, but knew that he didn't have a choice. If he wanted to save Charlee, then he would have to go see Tabakov Danilovich. But this visit wouldn't be for a business deal. No, West had something in his grasp that was more valuable than gold.

Charlee's life.

West pulled his cell phone from his pocket and dialed his secretary. He didn't care what time it was back home. He paid her good money to be available to him around the clock. She answered on the first ring.

"Find me Tabakov Danilovich and set up a meeting," he said and ended the call. Diana was one hell of an executive secretary, and he knew that even though the call was brief, he didn't have to repeat himself.

It was time for the Ruslanovich Bratva to pay their debt.

TWENTY THREE

Charlee groaned as she shifted in the plush bed that seemed to engulf her and take her hostage. Dr. Romanova had just left a few minutes ago after coming to check in on her and ensuring that she was comfortable. The slight dull pain pulsed in her left bicep, causing her to gasp as she attempted to sit up in the bed.

The worst of the pain seemed to be over. The pain medications Dr. Romanova prescribed appeared to be doing their job. Charlee reached for her pill bottle and glass of water, downing one of the pain pills. If she took two, she was sure to become drowsy. According to the Russian doctor, she was cleared to walk around the sanctuary's main buildings, but she could not go out into the field yet. She wanted Charlee to rest for a few more days.

This morning, she woke up to find West gone. At some point in the night, Malena must have left. She remembered the feel of his strong arms surrounding her and him placing a kiss at the base of her neck before she drifted off into her medicated slumber. It was his arms that kept the nightmares of the shooting at bay.

"Let me get dressed," she muttered, standing from the bed. A comfortable outfit was laid out on the chaise in the corner.

Malena.

"That woman knows me," she laughed, walking over to the bathroom.

She was not allowed a shower yet. Dr. Romanova didn't want the bandage and wound to get wet. She washed up as best she could at the sink, but her shoulder began to throb from the constant movement. She cursed, knowing that she was supposed to leave it in the sling, but how could she wash her body without moving it? She had to hit certain areas with soap and water!

"Hello!" Malena shouted from the bedroom.

"I'm in here," she answered with a grimace. She attempted to wrap the towel around her and failed.

"You should have waited until I came back," Malena scolded.

"You're not washing me. I love you, but I'm drawing the line at that," Charlee chuckled through her pain.

"Whatever." Malena waved her hand as Charlee walked out of the bathroom and over to the chaise. The towel slipped, but Charlee gave up. It wasn't like Malena hadn't seen her in the nude before.

"Sorry," Charlee said, reaching for her clean underwear. She struggled to put them on, but refused Malena's help again. She slid the leggings on, then looked at the bra.

Malena laughed at her with a pitiful look.

"It's not funny," Charlee muttered as her friend came over and assisted her with her bra and shirt. There was no way that she could walk around with no bra. The girls were bountiful, and had to be contained when in public.

"I don't know about you, but I'm famished," Malena announced as she adjusted Charlee's sling.

"Me too. Let's go downstairs and find food," Charlee suggested.

She was curious as to where West had disappeared to. She knew that he was pissed about the shooting, and she could tell that he was torn up on the inside about her pain. She didn't know how or why, but she could feel his emotions. No matter how many times she tried to convince him that it was not his fault that some idiot shot her, he still blamed himself.

Charlee and Malena made their way to the first floor of the building and followed the signs to the dining hall. Charlee's stomach grumbled with the smell of hot, fresh food. In the few weeks they had been in the wild, they didn't get this.

"Oh my, what is that smell?" Malena groaned, rubbing her abdomen as their steps quickened.

"I don't know, but it needs to get in my belly," Charlee laughed as they reached the dining area. Malena grabbed a tray and pushed Charlee over to the food line. Malena piled food on the tray for both of them. She carried it over to an empty table near a large window that allowed people to enjoy a meal and have a picture perfect view of nature.

Charlee grabbed her fork and took a few bites of her food. It was some native casserole dish, and was amazing. Taking a sip of her drink, she glanced around, and a familiar figure caught her eye out on the terrace. She grabbed her napkin and wiped her mouth.

West.

"I'll be back," she said, excusing herself from the table.

She adjusted the sling as she made her way toward him. She walked around a few tables, her eyes never leaving his muscular frame. Her breath caught in her throat as she paused in the doorway. He was speaking in Russian. The tone of his voice was fierce as she listened. It didn't take all her advanced degrees to sense that something was wrong. She didn't know what the hell he was saying, but it did something for her. Her core pulsed with his commanding tone.

Down, girl.

He turned, as if sensing someone behind him. His eyes deepened as they met hers. Her heart rate spiked with his one look. Her skin began to tingle as his eyes took their time assessing her. Her nipples pushed painfully against her bra with the memory of their last time together. He motioned for her to come to him. Her body, on autopilot, moved at his command. He brought her to his side as he finished his call.

"How are you feeling?" he asked, placing a kiss on her forehead.

"Better," she said, feeling comforted by his warm body. Just being around him seemed to brighten her day. But something was wrong. She didn't know what, but she knew that phone call held the answers to her questions. "What's wrong?"

His deep sigh confirmed her suspicions. He reached up and brushed a strand of hair from her face as she waited for him to answer.

"I need to leave the sanctuary…" he began, but paused.

"Okay." She nodded, waiting for him to continue.

"There's someone that I need to meet with." He looked over her shoulder and motioned for someone to come over.

A large familiar man stepped out onto the terrace, shutting the door. She remembered seeing him the at the small hotel back in Lyrino.

"What's going on?" she asked, looking from the newcomer back to West.

"This is Drago. He's my top security specialist. While I'm gone, he's going to assign someone to protect you."

"Protect me?" she gasped. "From what?"

"We have reason to believe that you getting shot in the rainforest was no accident. They were aiming for you," Drago announced.

"What? Who would want me dead?" she cried out, her free hand covering her mouth. Fear took hold of her as she thought back to the shooting. Had she not jumped when she did, the bullet that pierced her left arm could have easily pierced the left side of her chest, hitting her square in the heart.

"Don't worry about—"

"No, you don't get to tell me that someone wants me dead and then keep secrets. This is my life. Who the hell would want me dead?" she demanded, putting her hand on her waist.

"I'm trying to protect you," he snapped, frustration lining his face.

"Who?" she backed away from him, needing to put space between them. Hurt flashed in his eyes as she distanced herself from him. Her fear slowly morphed to anger at the thought of someone trying to kill her because of her life's mission to save entire animal species'.

He cursed and took a few steps away from her. She stared at his back until he turned back to her.

"She deserves to know, West," Drago spoke from behind Charlee. She nodded her head in agreement. It was her right to know who wanted her dead.

She held her breath as he stalked back to her with a dangerous gleam in his eye that she had never seen before. At least, not in a human. The same look in his eyes was that of a tiger on the hunt. She swallowed hard as he stopped in front of her, causing her to tilt her head back.

"The Ruslanovich Bratva have put a hit out on you," he announced, causing a gasp to escape her.

Her knees drew weak. The Russian Mafia? That anger she was experiencing immediately dissipated and fear slammed back into her chest. She swallowed a few times, trying to get words to form, but she couldn't. What the hell had she done to have a hit put out on her?

"I'm going to leave, and Drago's man will protect you," he instructed.

"Don't leave me," she cried out, panic filling her chest. She had watched enough mafia movies to know that having a hit out on a person was a death warrant already signed. He couldn't leave her. Not now. She wasn't expecting his announcement to take this route.

"You'll be fine," he stated, grabbing her by the shoulders as she shook her head. "I want you to carry a weapon on you. Do you think you can fire a handgun with only one hand?"

She jerked her head in a nod. Hell yeah, she would be able to shoot a gun. She didn't care what type of pain it caused. If it came down to it, she'd rip the damn sling off to be able to protect herself.

"Charlee," he snapped, gaining her attention as her imagination ran wild.

"Are they all like you?" she asked, waving a hand toward Drago.

"Yes, we are," Drago spoke up. She was slightly comforted, knowing that these men that would be protecting her were like West.

"Where are you going?" she asked, feeling the warm trail of tears along her cheeks. She blinked her eyes a few times to try to clear her vision.

She had never been so frightened in her life. She had been in the depths of dangerous jungles all over the world, and that was nothing compared to knowing that people were going to be hunting her down for the money.

"I'm going to go talk to the Ruslanovich pakhan." West rubbed her arms as he looked down at her.

"You know him?" She sniffed, leaning into his chest. This was turning into the worst nightmare of all. Never in a million years would she have ever believed that her life would be the backdrop of a real life movie.

"Unfortunately, I do," he answered as he rubbed her back. "My secretary has set up a meeting with him. A helicopter will be here shortly to pick me up."

"Don't worry, West. Ivan will guard her with his life while we're gone. Let's move to a more secured area where we can talk more," Drago suggested. "We need to discuss the plan, and out here is not the place to do so."

"I have the utmost confidence in Ivan." West's chest rumbled as he spoke. "But you're right. Let's go up to our suite to discuss details."

West guided her off the terrace and through the dining room with Drago leading the way. His hand at the small of her back provided reassurance. She caught Malena's curious eyes and motioned for her to follow them. Malena would never believe what she had to tell her.

Charlee briefly closed her eyes and sent up a silent prayer that Ivan would be as good as Drago was suggesting. She didn't need anyone dying for her. All she needed was for him to keep her alive and in one piece so that West could come back to her.

TWENTY FOUR

Diana had pulled off a miracle. He would make sure that she received extra on her bonus this year. He didn't know how the woman did what she did, but not only had she booked the meeting with Tabakov, she sent a helicopter with a mini wardrobe for him to have decent business attire for his meeting. Now that he knew Charlee was secure, he could concentrate. This meeting with the Ruslanovich pakhan would be one of the most important meetings of his life.

Tabakov was a shrewd businessman, but West wasn't worried. He knew that he too was a hard businessman, and he could handle the likes of

Tabakov. He refused to leave this meeting without his demands being met. The contract would be removed from Charlee's head.

He shifted in his seat as the pilot announced through their headphones that they would be coming upon their destination soon. They would be meeting Tabakov at his office in the city of Khabarovsk. It was one of the larger cities in Far East Russia, and just so happened to be less than twenty miles from the Chinese border.

West glanced out the window as they flew over the Amur River. The sun was slowly making its way down, drifting past the horizon. West wished he could have shared this moment with Charlee. Once they had reached the suite earlier, it was decided it would be best to move her. His thoughts turned to her concerned eyes as the black sedan carried her away.

He'd had to keep from jumping in the car with her. Her trusting eyes had gazed up at him with love before she got in the car. His tiger paced beneath his skin even now at the memory. She'd put her trust fully into him, and he would not let her down. Once he returned to her, he would let her know his true feelings. The entire world would come to know how Weston Rogavac felt about Dr. Charlee Black.

Now that they knew there was an official hit out on her, the sanctuary would not be safe. This trip to Far East Russia was well-publicized, and anyone with a smartphone would know how to locate her. Hit men would be coming out of the woodwork. So they moved her to a safe house deep in a shifter town, known as Sukhan.

Humans would be fools to attempt to harm her there. A few of his cousins and distant relatives lived in the town, and he trusted that they would protect her. Shifters tended to band together. Even though Charlee was not a shifter, the fact that he'd laid claim to her when making arrangements was good enough. No one would dare think twice about laying a hand on her while she was there. His family was royalty amongst the shifter world for everything that they had done for not only tigers, but other shifter groups around the world.

Claim her.

Just the thought of officially claiming her stirred his cock. His tiger too. His tiger ached to mark her as his. And he would. The minute he returned to her, she would receive his claiming mark and would be his forever. Now that the cat was literally out the bag, he would explain the claiming, and that they were meant to be together, forever. He knew that she had feelings for him, and he could admit that he was head over heels for her as well.

"Please prepare for descent." The pilot's words broke through West's thoughts. He glanced around and met the fierce gazes of Luka and Drago. He nodded to each, knowing that they were ready to walk straight into the belly of the beast with him.

The helicopter began to make its descent down to the landing pad in the small airport. West watched as a dark sedan drove up to wait for him. The whirl sounds of the blades filled the air as the pilot gently put the copter on the ground.

They quickly exited the helicopter and made their way over to the dark sedan. The driver stood by the opened back passenger door. West nodded to the driver as he entered the vehicle. It was time to go meet with the head of the Ruslanovich Bratva.

They had arrived. West's tiger growled as they entered the ancient building in what was known as the downtown of Khabarovsk. Three large human security guards in black suits stood from behind their security posts to greet them.

"Mr. Danilovich has been expecting you, Mr. Rogavac," the first guard announced in Russian as he walked from behind the desk.

West's animal was instantly on alert. He glanced around the lobby of the building, taking in the old rustic decor that was updated, yet still held an old-world charm to the building. It was nothing like the modern office building that Tabakov owned in Moscow that stretched high up into the clouds.

"I'm glad to know that Tabakov is sending down a welcome committee," West stated, speaking in his native tongue.

"But of course," the second guard stated. "For safety reasons. Hope you do not mind." The guard waved the security wands in front of him.

West's tiger growled low, but he knew that neither of them had weapons on them. But if it made the humans feels safe, so be it. He kept his cool about him as they walked around them, waving the wands around their bodies to check for anything metal. He didn't shy away from the humans as they made sure that no weapons would enter into the Russian business establishment.

"Thank you for your patience," the first guard said. West didn't like the tone in the man's voice, but he would let it slide for now. He was not who West needed to see, and he had more pressing things to worry about than knocking the smirk off the guard's face.

They were then escorted over to the elevators. The six of them were a little too close for comfort in the elevator. Drago ensured that he was directly behind Luka and West as they rode up the elevator in an uncomfortable silence, up to the fourth floor.

Once the doors opened, West relaxed slightly as they silently walked down a hallway toward a reception desk. West took note that there were no other humans around. Granted, it was after hours, but he found it weird that there weren't even signs of a cleaning service.

"Mr. Rogavac is here to see, Mr. Danilovich," the first guard announced as they reached the desk. She motioned for them to have a seat while she picked up the phone. She was a slightly older woman, with blonde hair painfully pulled back into a bun. Her suit looked sharp and fresh. Neither West, Luka, or Drago moved to have a seat. They would stand. She briefly spoke into the phone, announcing their arrival.

"He will be with you shortly," she informed them before going back to typing on her computer. West glanced around at Luka and Drago, who had yet to take their eyes off the guards. The guards were not making any excuses for openly staring at them. They may have checked them for weapons, but West was certain that each of the human guards had at least one weapon on them. Not that West, Luka, or Drago had anything to worry about. The human bullets would do little to nothing to a shifter.

It didn't take long before the phone next to the receptionist rang. She promptly answered it, listened, and hung up before turning her sharp features toward West.

"Mr. Danilovich will see you now, Mr. Rogavac," she stated as she turned back to her computer.

"Please, this way." The guard waved his hand, indicating for West to follow him.

"Only Mr. Rogavac may enter the office, gentlemen," the second guard announced as he and the third guard blocked Luka and Drago's path. West shook his head at them. He would not need them in the room for what he had to discuss with Tabakov.

"I'll be fine," West assured them, with a hand raised in the air to stop Drago's protest. He knew that if he really needed them, there wasn't a person in the room who could hold back two ferocious tigers. He followed the guard toward a solid oak door. He held it open for West to allow him entrance.

West entered the office and found its decor dark and masculine. The sound of the door closing behind him caused him to turn. The guard did not enter, but West was sure that he was standing outside the door. The wall to wall windows gave a breathtaking view of the town. West looked around and found himself to be alone. He took his time walking over to the window to admire the view.

The muffled sound of a toilet flushing filled the air, followed by the sound of running water. West's shifter hearing picked up on movement in the bathroom before the door opened. He turned and found Tabakov Danilovich striding toward him. He was of medium height for a human, with an athletic build. His blond hair held a touch of gray on the sides. He offered a smile that West was sure he thought was warm and welcoming, but West saw immediately through the pakhan's facade.

"Weston, how have you been? Beautiful view, isn't it?" Tabakov asked, his hand outstretched. West gripped his hand in a tight, firm handshake, grateful that the mafia boss had decided to wash his hands before exiting the facilities. "Wow, strong grip you have there."

"I'm fine. How have you been?" West asked in Russian as he followed Tabakov over to his desk. He took a seat in the plush leather chair across from Tabakov's desk while the pakhan settled into his chair.

"Business is going well," he said. "I was a little surprised to see that you were requesting a meeting with me. It's been too long since we last spoke, but I would be interested in any business proposal that Rogavac Industries would be willing to present."

"I'm not here on official Rogavac Industries business," West announced, trying to tame his tiger. His animal paced, not liking the too smooth front that the pakhan was presenting. He was a snake in the grass, just waiting to strike.

"Oh, no?" Tabakov tried to appear shocked, but West knew that it was a front.

"Cut the bullshit," West snapped, calling his bluff. "I know that the Ruslanovich Bratva has been keeping an eye on what's going on over in Siberia at the Panthera National Park, and I know that your Bratva has a hand in the poaching business."

"What do you want me to say?" Tabakov asked, the smile vanishing from his face. A cold, hard mask swept across the pakhan's features. "I am a businessman, and there is much money to be had in that business. There are plenty of private collectors who are willing to pay top dollar for the merchandise that my organization can offer them. And yes, I knew that you and your little SPAT organization was running around the Far East, trying to save your precious tigers."

"You're talking about a business that would wipe out an entire species," West growled. His tiger was restless, begging to be let out, but West pushed him down.

Not now.

"You Rogavac's waste too much money trying to save the world and your precious animals. There is so much more that you could do with your money," Tabakov stated, leaning back in his chair.

"What we do with our money is none of your concern," West snapped, irritation lining his voice. "I also know that you have put a hit out on Dr. Charlee Black."

Tabakov's eyes widened, the disgust at the mention of Charlee's name was apparent on his face.

"Don't worry about Dr. Black. She's a dime a dozen, and there will be someone else soon."

Charlee, a dime a dozen?

Not hardly. She was priceless. Irreplaceable.

She was his.

"Tabakov, it's time that a Rogavac claimed the favor that was promised by your grandfather to mine."

"What?" Tabakov sputtered, his face flushing red.

Anger spewed from his eyes, but West didn't care. He knew that the Russian would have to honor it. The Ruslanovich Bratva was like any other brotherhood. Honor was a code that they lived by. It would bring dishonor to his family if he did not abide by the promise that was made from his grandfather.

Whenever a Rogavac calls on a Ruslanovich, they would honor any requests.

TWENTY FIVE

Tabakov scowled as he stared down West. The tiger in West was brimming near the surface and he was sure that the Russian could see it.

"How can I call off a hit?" Tabakov asked, waving his hand in the air. "It's not like I just told one person. It doesn't work that way. The announcement of the hit went out in the network. There will be at least fifty men gunning for her."

West snapped, his beast slamming into his chest. Nothing would happen to Charlee. West flew from his chair and dragged the mafia boss from his chair. His breaths came fast and hard as he held the pakhan in the air with one hand. He was fighting for control of his animal, and was currently losing the battle.

"You will honor the request and kill the hit," West growled around his fangs that had descended against his will. Tabakov struggled to break free, but was no match for the strength of West and his tiger. If he had to beat it out of the Russian mafia boss, he would take great pleasure.

Tabakov's eyes widened at the sight of West's massive canines.

"I know what you and your family are," Tabakov sputtered. West tightened his grip and brought him closer to his face.

"Then you know that you had better honor the request of a Rogavac as your grandfather promised." West tossed Tabakov to the floor.

West made no excuse to what he was. He was a proud shifter. He was glad that the Russian knew exactly who and what he was dealing with. It wasn't like he could run around telling the world. His fellow humans would call him crazy, as he wouldn't have any proof. Humans were still ignorant to the fact that others lived among them. So no, West was not afraid that the Russian Mafia boss would tell anyone.

Tabakov laid there, trying to catch his breath. West pulled back on his tiger, unwilling to let the tiger break free. If it did come to the forefront, there would be no help for Tabakov. His tiger was in a frenzy, knowing that there was a threat to Charlee, and it would attack the human in front of him.

"Why are you protecting her? What is she to you?" Tabakov asked, his voice strained.

West stood over him, looking down at the man in disgust. It was this man's fault that Charlee was shot at twice. Not just in the jungle, but back on the train also. He knelt down next to the mafia boss with a stare that he knew revealed his animal. Fear permeated the air as Tabakov tried to scoot away, but his back hit the desk.

"All you need to know is that she's with me. Any harm comes to her again and I will be the one hunting you down. The Bratva are not the only ones that can make a person disappear," West threatened in a low growl.

Commotion could be heard outside the office door. West glanced at the door and was confident that Drago and Luka had full control of the situation.

"Now answer me," he growled, turning back to the disheveled Tabakov. "Are you going to honor your family's promise?"

"Yes," Tabakov conceded, breathing heavily. "I will call it off. I just pray that it isn't too late."

"You better hope it's not." West stood and walked toward the door. "If it is, nothing will protect you from my tiger. He's not as nice and forgiving as me."

"How's your pain?" Malena asked, concern lining her face as she settled on the couch next to Charlee.

"I'm okay. It's just a little achy right now," Charlee answered, adjusting the sling. With all the adrenaline coursing through her, she barely felt the pain.

The house they were brought to was located in the small town of Kutsk. Ivan had assured her that it was where West had wanted her taken. It was a safe town, and any person would be a fool to try to mess with her. The tiny home wasn't much bigger than her office at the university. Small open floor plan with the living room and kitchen in one space, a bedroom, and a tiny bathroom. It didn't leave much room for three adults to function in the tiny efficiency home.

When they had left the sanctuary, they'd only had time to hastily grab a few outfits before being ushered into a dark sedan. Charlee had been unable to tell Malena much. All that was said was someone was trying to kill Charlee and that they must move her. Malena, being the best friend that she was, didn't question anything. Her bag was packed in record time. That's why Charlee loved her friend so much.

"I'm going to go look around outside," Ivan said, leaving from his perch by the window.

"Are you sure it's needed? I thought you said this town would be safe?" Charlee asked as she watched him come to her. He pulled out a small automatic weapon, checked the clip, then held it out to her.

Ivan was a man of few words. Within moments of being in his presence, she knew that she and Malena would be safe. Nothing got past him. He took his job very seriously. No smiles. No jokes. His words were instructions. Since they had relocated into the house, he had drilled into their brains where the keys to the car were, always be prepared for anything, emergency exits, and always sleep with decent clothes on, just in case they had to leave in a hurry.

She could see the tiger in him with every move. It was amazing that no one else could see it. She saw the same in West, Luka, and Drago. Every movement that they made was just as graceful as a tiger in the wild. Was it only because she was privileged to know the secret that she could see it? Or was it just so apparent that everyone else ignored it?

"We can never be too sure," he stated as she took the gun in her right hand. It was lightweight, and she knew that she wouldn't have any issues using it. "If I'm not back in fifteen minutes and someone comes through the door, shoot first and ask questions later."

"What if it's you?" Malena asked wide-eyed.

He released a snort as he walked to the door. "Shoot first, ask questions later." And then he was gone.

Charlee knew his reasoning behind the snort. The bullets would do nothing to him. West had begun to teach her of his world whenever they were alone. He had explained to her that the night she discovered his secret, if she would have pulled the trigger while his chest was pressed against her gun, it would have burned and hurt, but due to his shifter genes, his body would have begun to instantly heal.

"What's his deal?" Malena asked, turning to Charlee. She didn't know what to say. She tucked the gun into the side of the cushion of the couch while she tried to think of something good to say. She couldn't tell her best friend that if she did accidentally shoot him, it would do nothing to him but piss him off.

"I don't know." Charlee shrugged. "West and Luka trust him, and he has given his word to keep us safe, so that's all that matters."

"You're right." Malena sighed, leaning back on the couch. "Now that we're finally alone, you must tell me everything. Why is someone trying to kill you? Why are we in a safe house in some small town? I feel like we're in the middle of an action-packed suspense movie and I can't figure out the plot."

"You and me both," Charlee scoffed. Only this movie is mixed with a hint of the paranormal world, she thought to herself. "Well, I didn't know that the shooter was gunning for me." She began the story, telling Malena everything that she was told on the terrace. Malena sat, mouth wide open as she continued the story, and where exactly West was now.

She knew that he was off meeting with the mafia boss, the same one that wanted her dead. She put on a brave face, but truth be told, she was scared shitless. What if the mafia boss wouldn't call off the hit? What if he hurt West or worse, kill him? She'd seen enough mafia movies with her brother, Dane, to know how this could turn out.

"Then you know the rest," she concluded, feeling spent. A yawn escaped her as she looked at the time. It was late, and there was no telling when West would return.

"He isn't back yet," Malena announced nervously.

Shit.

Charlee reached for the firearm by her leg and felt somewhat comforted as the cool steel.

"I'm sure everything is fine," Charlee murmured, trying to believe her own words.

"Should we go look for him?" Malena barked out a nervous laugh, but Charlee knew she was not making this a laughing matter at all.

"Hell no," Charlee said, just as the sound of a key in the door filled the air. She whipped out the gun, flipping the safety off. She winced from the dull pain in her left arm as she stood slowly and took aim at the door. Malena drew quiet as they both waited to see who would come through the door.

Finally, the door opened and in walked Ivan, who looked disgruntled. She relaxed and dropped the gun to her side.

"I thought I said shoot first—"

"I was going to make it a head shot," she said, interrupting him. "I figured I'd better make it count."

He finally cracked a small smile as he closed and locked the door behind him. "I knew I liked you," he said as he went back to the window seat.

"Thank you?" She wasn't sure if it was a compliment, but she had a feeling that was the closest thing to one from this man.

"It's getting late. You two had better get some rest. West and the others are due to return tomorrow."

"Have you heard anything?" she asked as Malena headed into the bedroom.

"No, but we weren't expecting to either. Go," he said gently. "Get some rest. West will have my head if you're not taken care of properly. Keep the gun with you. I'll be going out again to check the perimeter, and next time, I mean it. Shoot first and ask questions later."

TWENTY SIX

Charlee's eyes snapped open. She wasn't sure what woke her. She turned and found Malena softly snoring on her side of the bed. Her body relaxed slightly, but something still bothered her. She didn't want to wake Malena if it was nothing. She laid still at first, straining to hear if it was a noise or something out in the living room. It was probably Ivan moving around.

Then she remembered.

He'd never made a noise in the house.

Something was wrong. The hairs on her arms stood at attention and she knew that she had to investigate what had woke her. She slowly sat up, her heart slamming against her chest. She threw her legs over the side of the bed and pushed her hair out of her face. As Ivan instructed, she had left her shoes by the side of the bed. She slipped on the comfortable tennis shoes and reached for the weapon on the side table. Gently pushing off the bed, she tapped Malena on the foot to wake her.

She made it to the door and slowly cracked it open. Her eyes had to adjust to the darkness as she waited. She could hear Malena crawling out of the bed, and nothing seemed to be out of the ordinary. She could not see Ivan and figured he must have went out on patrol. She blew out a deep breath, but then paused. Her eyes widened as she watched the door slowly open and a figure slowly crept into the house.

It was certainly not Ivan.

Even in the dark, she could see that the figure was a few inches shorter than Ivan. The moonlight reflected off the large knife that he held in his hand.

Where was Ivan?

Her heart pounded in her chest. There was only one other way out of the house and that was through the window in their bedroom. Charlee glanced at Malena who was standing behind her. She signaled that there was one person making his way toward them. She tried to close the door quietly, but she was too late.

He spotted her.

She slammed the door shut and flipped the lock, but it was old and would not hold the assailant as he slammed into the door. It shook the hinges as he tried to force his way in. She ignored the pain as she lifted her arms and aimed her weapon at the door.

"The window!" Malena shouted, rushing over to open it. Charlee slowly backed up toward Malena, but refused to take her eyes off the door.

Malena jumped up and began crawling through it, just as the door gave way. Charlee didn't hesitate as she fired the gun as the assailant made his way into the room. His body jerked back. He tried to move forward again, but she pulled the trigger again. This time, his body fell to the ground.

She didn't wait to see if he would get up. She turned and hoisted her way out of the window. Her arm began to burn, but she ignored it as she jumped down from the windowsill. It would have to wait until they could get to safety.

"Are you okay?" Malena whispered as they made their way to the back of the house. They quickly followed the instructions that Ivan had drilled into them when he went over escape plans. Stay in the shadows. She never would have thought that they would have to use them.

"Yeah," Charlee whispered back as she gripped the gun tight. Even if her arm was falling off, she wouldn't admit that the pain was becoming unbearable. Her main focus was finding Ivan. But she knew, after the way he drilled the emergency plan into their brain, what they needed to do.

Get to the car and get the hell out of there.

They quickly made their way to their parked car three houses away in complete silence. She could tell that Malena was running on adrenaline. She would go through her shock later. It wasn't like her to be so quiet, but at a time like this, silence was a must. Charlee gripped the gun tight in her hand to keep it from shaking.

They finally made their way to the dark sedan. Malena jumped into the driver's seat while Charlee slid into the passenger seat, holding in a grimace.

"Where the hell is Ivan?" Malena asked, turning the car on and yanking it into drive.

"I don't know. But you know what he said, we have to get to the next house." She gasped as the pain began to settle in.

"You're hurting!" Malena cursed and punched the gas. Charlee grimaced as she jerked back in her seat. She closed her eyes for a brief moment, trying to get the pain under control. Malena released a scream and slammed on the breaks.

Charlee's eyes flew open as she stared at the figure in the headlights.

Ivan.

Charlee could see dark stains on his clothing and knew that it was blood. The only question was, whose blood was it? He stalked toward the car, but didn't appear to be injured.

Just pissed off.

Malena opened the driver's side door and scrambled into the back seat to allow him to get in the car.

"Where were you?" Charlee demanded to know as he pulled off.

"Ran into a little trouble," he said, jerking the car down a narrow road.

"Well so did we," Malena shouted from the back seat.

"I know. I found the dead body when I made it back to the house. You girls did good," he announced, glancing over at Charlee.

Seeing her pain, he let loose a string of curses.

She turned her head and peered out the window as the darkened skyline flew past. She focused on the moon to try to block out the pain. Her body leaned toward the door as Ivan made a sharp left.

She wondered where West was and if he was okay. All that she wanted right now was him by her side. She needed to be able to feel him next to her and assure that everything was okay.

"Hold on. We're almost there," Ivan stated.

"Charlee." Malena leaned forward and brushed her hair away from her face. "It'll be okay. West is going to take care of this."

"I know," Charlee whispered, knowing that he was going to try to do everything in his power to call off the hit. He had promised, and she would hold him to it.

West cursed as he disconnected the call. His first instinct was to crush his cellphone in his hand, but that wouldn't do him any good. He wouldn't be able to receive direct updates from Ivan. Ivan just informed him of the trouble that they ran in to in the small cottage. It should have been safe and quiet, but it would seem that the hit men that Tabakov hired were extremely good at their job of hunting people down.

Ivan informed him that while out patrolling around the perimeter of the property, he came across two men. While dealing with them, a third managed to sneak into the cottage with the girls. Ivan's discovery of the body of the third assassin with two bullets to the chest made West's chest fill with pride.

His mate was a force to be reckoned with. His tiger was pleased that she was able to protect not only herself, but her best friend, while following the instructions that Ivan had drilled into their heads.

"Two bullets to the heart." Ivan's words echoed in his head.

His mate was for sure a dead shot. It made him take note to never get on her bad side while she had a gun in her presence.

He radioed in to the pilot of the chopper. "How much longer until we're there?"

"About twenty minutes, sir," the pilot responded.

They were on their way back to Kutsk. Now, after speaking to Ivan, he knew that it was imperative that they get to Charlee soon. If Tabakov was not able to cancel the hit, then he would have to answer to West. By the time West left the Russian pakhan's place of business, they had an understanding. If one hair was harmed on Charlee Black's head, Weston Rogavac would be hunting down the leader of the Ruslanovich Bratva.

"Did everyone make it from the safe house uninjured?" Luka asked quietly from his position in the helicopter.

"So far. The girls were shaken up, but otherwise fine. Ivan said that he could see that Charlee was in pain, but she hasn't complained once," he said, staring out the chopper's window. His cat was pleased that their mate was such a trooper.

Mate.

He had to get used to using that term for Charlee. His cat had definitely made up his mind, and a shifter's animal was never wrong when it came to finding their other half.

West couldn't wait for the chopper to land. He desperately needed to get to her side so that he could see with his own eyes that she was okay. Drago sat across from him on the phone, arranging for more men to head to the area of the second safe house. There was no telling how much action was headed their way.

The sound of his cellphone ringing broke through his thoughts. He glanced down at the glass screen and saw his mother's name come across. He paused, tempted to ignore the call, but knew that Inez Rogavac would continue to call until she got through to him.

"Hello," he answered.

"West, thank God!" Inez exclaimed, sounding breathless. His tiger perked up at the sound of her voice. Inez Rogavac was a very distinguished woman, a high figure in the shifter community. Panic in her voice was unusual.

"Mother, what is it?" he asked, sitting up in his seat. His imagination began to run wild with the possibilities of something happening to his mother. If Tabakov reneged on their deal—

"What is going on over there? It's made national news that Dr. Charlee Black was injured at the sanctuary, and now she and her assistant are missing!"

West settled back and blew out his breath. His mother was okay. He should have known that what was going on at the sanctuary would leak to the news. The news stations were all over the mission before they arrived there. He should have known that snatching Charlee and moving her would create a stir.

"Do you know what happened? You were there too! How could you let something like this happen to them? You know how much she means to the shifter community for all of her work for the tigers—"

"Mother, they're okay," he cut her off. Silence met him on the phone. "Charlee and Malena are safe."

"Well, what in the world is going on? They're saying that she was shot by a poacher and was recovering, then they both disappeared!"

"It wasn't just any poacher, Mother. I moved them to keep them safe. We're the only ones that can keep Charlee safe right now." He turned to stare out at the clouds as the chopper broke through them.

"What are you talking about?" his mother asked.

"I had to go to the Ruslanovich Bratva. They had a hit out on Charlee," he admitted.

West couldn't believe his ears as his mother released a curse. Inez Rogavac was a lady, and ladies just did not use profanity. It was unladylike.

"West, for you to go to that Bratva, that means something. What is she to you? We Rogavac's have never had to pull out the favor card. It's been decades since that promise was made to your grandfather. Why now? Why would you go to them and request a favor?" she demanded.

Inez may be a distinguished woman in the shifter community, but she could be fierce when needed. The sound of her voice now reminded him of his childhood when he and his brother, Major, would be in a world of trouble. They loved testing their mother back then, just to get under her skin.

"Weston," she snapped impatiently.

"She's my mate," he shouted. He felt the eyes of Drago and Luka on him and knew that he had just let the cat out of the bag. But he wouldn't take it back. His mother deserved to know his reasoning behind going to the Bratva. If Tabakov didn't hold up his part of the deal, it would bring shame to him and his family. Honor was something that the Bratva lived by.

"She's your mate?" Her voice softened.

"Yes, ma'am," he answered, his eyes moving to Luka. His friend nodded. No words needed to be said between them. A shifter's mate was to be protected, and he knew that his best friend would do what was needed to help keep Charlee safe, even if it meant declaring war between tiger shifters around the world and the Ruslanovich Bratva.

"Do what you must to keep her safe. I can't wait to finally meet my future daughter-in-law."

"Yes, ma'am," he assured.

He would end this, one way or another. Charlee Black would make her way safely home and stay in his arms forever.

TWENTY SEVEN

Charlee paced the small sitting room of West's cousin Grekov's home. Midmorning and she hadn't got an ounce of sleep since waking in the middle of the night. Time had flown by in a blur. By the time they had settled in Grekov's home, she couldn't sleep. Malena, on the other hand, was snoring quietly on the couch as Charlee thought of her situation.

Ivan's deep voice could be heard in the foyer speaking to a few men who had shown up. She had no clue who they were. She had yet to even meet

West's cousin Grekov. He was not home when they arrived. Charlee was impressed with his house after the little cottage they had been holed up in before.

"You're going to wear a path in the wood floors," Malena announced sleepily from the couch.

"How long does it take to talk a mafia boss out of a hit?" Charlee wondered as she turned toward her friend.

"He'll come for you," Malena declared as she sat up on the couch. "I'm actually quite jealous of the sparks that fly between the two of you. And by the looks that he gives you, he won't be giving you up anytime soon."

"I'm just worried about him. Who can just walk up to the Russian Mafia and demand for a hit to be cancelled?"

"Charlee, please, stop pacing. You're looking like a cat trapped in a cage. Please come sit next to me." Malena patted the spot next to her.

Charlee hadn't even realized that she had started pacing again, as she was lost in her thoughts. She made her way to Malena and sat, tucking her legs beneath her. Worry filled her chest as her mind began to wander. Why hadn't West called her to check on her? Was something wrong? What if the Russian Mafia killed him? Why would they stop a hit because of him? He didn't hold that much power.

Or did he?

"I just don't like this feeling. The unknown, you know?" She turned to Malena as panic started to set in. "I killed someone last night. I've shot a gun plenty of times, but at animals. I killed a human. Someone's brother, father, son—"

"And that someone was trying to kill you," Ivan said from the doorway. He leaned against the doorjamb, his intense eyes boring into hers. "It was him or you. Believe me when I say that he had every intention of walking out of there to collect the bounty on your head. He was not going to think twice of killing you."

"But it's—"

He held up his hand and cut her off. She took a deep breath, trying to calm her nerves.

"He's right, Charlee." Malena nodded. "He was coming to murder you. You were a paycheck for him."

Charlee sighed and leaned back into the plush couch. In the back of her mind, she knew that they were both right, but it still weighed heavily on her that she took a life.

"With it being daytime, we should be safe. No one would try to kill me in the daytime, would they?" she asked, turning to Ivan. She just couldn't imagine assassins making their plans to kill someone in broad daylight.

"These are hard core killers you're talking about. They don't care that it's daytime or nighttime. They're trying to collect a bounty that has been offered for your death. Forget anything that you may have seen in the movies. These men are the real deal. They will stop at nothing to kill you," he said, folding his arms in front of his chest.

Her small bubble of hope burst with his words as her fear escalated. She just hoped that everything would be okay with it being daylight, buying her time until West could return to her. She reached up a shaky hand and tucked her thick hair behind her ear.

"Shit," she murmured. It was the only response that she could come up with. She turned to Malena and found that her wide eyes mirrored the fear that filled Charlee. She closed her eyes and wished that she was back home, relaxing over a long weekend before returning to teach her beloved students.

"Just relax. You can move around the house, but you can't leave the building. There are a few more men that have been assigned to help secure the premises. We'll be ready for anything this time."

"West sent them?" she asked. Her heart skipped a beat with the thought that he was trying to keep her protected while he was away.

"Yes. This should all be over soon." He nodded before walking away from the door.

"Soon we'll be able to go home," Malena said with a yawn. She snuggled down on the couch, pulling her blanket over her.

"How can you sleep at a time like this?" Charlee slapped at Malena's feet that tried to burrow beneath her leg.

"My body is running on fumes." Malena yawned again. "We're safe now. We just have to wait for your knight in shining armor to come rescue us."

"Fine! Go to sleep. I'm going to look around the house." Charlee stood from the couch. She was restless and needed to do something. She left out of the sitting room and wandered down the hallway, figuring that she would explore the house. It was a beautiful home, and the owner had yet to come home.

She pushed down the fear that was consuming her with the thought that she was in a member of West's family home. Hopefully, she would get to meet Grekov. His home was beautiful, and the character of the house spoke volumes about the owner. She made her way to the kitchen, loving the openness and the all glass windows that displayed the yard. She walked over to the window and sat on the window seat.

The property was secluded and was perfect for a tiger to roam. The biologist in her assessed the land, finding it open and with a dense forest that lined the property. She knew that this home and land were perfect for someone who had a tiger in them that needed to roam. A movement in the woods caught her attention. She paused, not knowing what it was. She leaned forward, straining to see, and then she saw it.

Gun.

She let loose a scream, just as a rain of bullets shattered the windows in front of her.

West stared out the car window as the scenery flew past. They had finally arrived to Kutsk and would soon arrive to Grekov's home. His cousin was out of town, but had opened his home to West for the safety of his mate. His tiger was anxious to get to Charlee. It paced back and forth, needing to put his eyes on her to ensure that she was safe and unharmed from the attack.

Once the hit was officially null and void, Tabakov would contact West. Tabakov would not want to see West again if something were to happen to Charlee. West was not joking when he threatened the pakhan. His tiger would not be as forgiving as the human counterpart.

"So she's your mate?" Luka's voice broke through West's thoughts. West glanced at his best friend and nodded. Just the sound of someone else referring to Charlee as his mate had his cat purring.

"She is," West confirmed.

"Are you going to teach her our ways and make it official?" Luka asked.

"I am. I believe that her feelings run as deep for me as mine do for her. Even though it's only been a short time, my tiger is sure." West looked to his friends, and both of them nodded in understanding. He was confident that his tiger would never steer him wrong.

The sound of a text message notification filled the air. They all reached for their phones, but it was Drago who sat in the passenger seat next to the driver who received the message. West's eyes flew to Drago as he cursed.

"What is it?" West asked, leaning forward as dread slowly filled his stomach. He didn't want to hear what Drago was going to say. He knew instantly it wasn't good.

"The house is under attack." Drago looked up from his phone with a solemn look.

"How bad is it?" West growled as his tiger paced inside of him, demanding to be let out.

"Full fledge attack." Drago's voice was low as he responded.

The contract was still active.

West's tiger slammed into his chest, not wanting to take no for an answer. Drago instructed the driver to push the car faster. They were less than ten minutes from his cousin's home.

It was the longest ten minutes of West's life. Every situation he could have imagined passed through his mind. He sent up a prayer that Charlee was unharmed. He couldn't imagine anything else. Just the thought that she was laying somewhere injured had his tiger clawing to get out. They arrived at the house and took in the battle scene. Smoke was streaming out of the back of his cousin's home.

The car came to a screeching halt at the base of the driveway. West exited the vehicle and could no longer control his animal. His tiger burst forward. He dropped to the ground as his body began the swift transformation. The sounds of his clothing shredding faded to the background as he let loose a fierce roar. His cat was pissed and demanding blood. He took off, running toward the house as the sounds of gunfire echoed throughout the air, but his focus was on finding Charlee.

A figure stepped out of the woods with an automatic rifle trained at the house. He didn't see the large tiger storming his way until it was too late. Surprise flashed across the man's face as West's tiger pounced on him. The screams of the assassin were drowned out as West sunk his canines into his throat.

The man's coppery fluid filled West's mouth as he snatched his teeth out of the throat. Gurgles filled the air, but West didn't wait around to see if death claimed him.

The sounds of gunfire grew louder, gaining his attention. He had to find Charlee. His tiger snapped and took off toward the gunfire. He found the back of the house engulfed in flames and the yard filled with humans pouring out of the woods, their automatic weapons trained on the house. Two other tigers appeared, rounding the corner of the other side of the house.

West roared, announcing the alpha's arrival, gaining the attention of the humans. More shifters began to appear from the woods behind the humans. The gunfire halted as the humans stood stunned. The men began to panic as they realized that they were surrounded. They quickly turned, looking for a way to escape, but there was nowhere for them to go. Tigers, wolves, and even a bear appeared from the trees.

The shifters of Kutsk had arrived. West planted his paws firmly on the ground in a defensive stance, ready to charge the humans. It would not end well for them. Some of them raised their rifles at the shifters and West braced himself. Their bullets would not slow down any of the shifters. It would just piss them off, so they had better make sure their shots counted.

"Drop your weapons!" Drago shouted from behind West.

"Fuck no! Do you see these fucking animals?" a male shouted back.

"Lower your weapons. These animals will not hurt you," Drago warned, walking toward the humans. He walked past West with a cellphone in his hand. "We know who you're after and the contract is now null and void. Cancelled. Walk away now and you will not be harmed."

West growled, knowing that he would not have promised that. His eyes roamed around the property, and each shifter was ready to attack. He was sure that they all had heard that these men were here to kill an innocent human.

His human.

They didn't deserve to live. They all deserved to die for even stepping foot on the property and trying to get to Charlee.

TWENTY EIGHT

Charlee sat in the corner of the small panic room in Grekov's home. She brought her knees up to her chest. Once the bullets had went flying, she had run back into the main part of the house. Even though they had only been in the house for a few hours, Ivan had drilled the escape plan into their heads for there as well.

"If shit jumps off, you're to run into the safe room and not open the door for anyone," were his exact instructions.

"Why would a person need a panic room?" Malena asked as she sat in the chair in front of the television monitors.

"I have no idea, but I'm glad that he does," she murmured, laying her head on her knees. Her arm didn't even bother her anymore. She must have been running on pure adrenaline.

Charlee was shook up. Again, someone had tried to kill her. This time, she saw the bullets coming. There was no doubt that they were trying to kill her. She was absolutely terrified. She wrapped her arms around her knees and drew them in tighter to her chest.

"These monitors aren't showing me what's going on outside of the house. All the video feeds are coming from inside the house," Malena disclosed with a heavy sigh.

The panic room was hidden behind a fake wall in Grekov's office. Once the heavy steel doors slammed shut behind them, they were sealed into the one hundred square foot room. It was outfitted with television monitors, a large cot, and a fridge stocked with food and water that would last them for a few days. It would take a tank to get through the steel walls and door of the room.

Charlee sighed deeply, not knowing what to think. Malena must have picked up on her emotions.

"Are you okay?" Malena asked, coming to kneel in front Charlee.

"I can't live the rest of my life this way," she admitted, her voice full with emotions. With the current attack, she felt defeated. She'd had high hopes that the contract would be cancelled. Panic began to rise in her chest. How would she ever lead a normal life? She'd always have to look over her shoulder in fear that someone was trying to kill her.

"Don't give up. West will succeed. He has to," Malena encouraged, grabbing her hands in hers. The faint hint of smoke came through the air vents, causing her panic to slam harder against her chest. What if they couldn't be rescued? What if the house burned to the ground with them in the panic room?

"But what if he can't? Seriously, Malena. Think of what my life would be dwindled down to. I would never be able to teach again. I couldn't be a biologist, something that I have dedicated my entire life to."

A warm trail of tears flowed down her cheeks. She angrily brushed them away. It wasn't her fault. All of this was because some thug wanted to kill her beloved tigers and wanted her out of the way so that they could make millions off of dead animals.

"Hey! Snap out of it," Malena demanded. "You aren't dead yet, but we will fight to the death. We're not going to just roll over and let them take us out. I always wanted to be able to have people tell stories about my death. If they break through the walls, we can grab the guns we have and go out in a blaze of glory, just like in the movies."

Charlee couldn't help but chuckle at the imagery of them shooting their way out of the panic room.

"You're crazy, you know that, right?" Charlee smiled. "First off, the steel doors can withstand ten thousand pounds of pressure. Don't you remember Ivan's lecture? I highly doubt that those men will be able to get in here," Charlee pointed out. She had to give it to the man, he was very thorough at his job and took it very seriously.

"All the more reason for you to be able to have a happy ending. You'll get West and you'll hook me up with one of his sexy friends. Or a brother. Please tell me he has a brother." Malena batted her eyes innocently.

"He does have a brother." Charlee chuckled at Malena's squeal of delight. Charlee reached out and grabbed Malena's hands again. What would she do without her? She never wanted to find out. "You know I love you, right?"

"I love you too, Charlee," Malena whispered. "We're all allowed a weak moment. You just need a kick in the ass to bring you back to your normal self and that's what I'm here for."

Charlee nodded her head, unable to speak as emotions overcame her. She watched as Malena went back to the chair in front of the monitors. She wiped her face to erase any evidence of her tears. The smell of smoke grew stronger and she didn't want to let on to Malena that it worried her. They were locked away in this steel framed room and the house could be burning down around them for all they knew.

"Here we are. I can see outside the house. It was just a click of the..." Malena paused, frozen in her chair.

Charlee slowly stood from her position and inched her way toward the monitors, but she already knew why her friend couldn't speak. Her eyes were just as captivated by what was on the screen as Malena's.

Tigers, wolves, and even a bear lined the property, surrounding men that were aiming guns at the home. Malena brought up different angles of the property and each showed animals behind the humans who were attacking. They couldn't hear what was going on, but Charlee knew that those animals were not just any ordinary animals.

They were shifters.

"Oh my," Charlee murmured as her eyes scanned the screen, desperate to see if any of the tigers were West. The smoke began to fill the small room through the air vents, throwing them both into a fit of coughing.

"What in the world—" Malena gasped. "I've never seen anything like this before. This is amazing. It's as if the animals are banding together against the men."

Charlee's eyes began to water as they watched in stunned silence as a large man walked from the direction of the front of the house. Charlee peered closer to the screen, recognizing Drago. He was speaking fiercely to the humans, but it didn't look like the men were going to budge.

Her lungs began to burn from the inhalation of smoke. She shot a glance at Malena and knew that she was worried now too. They both kneeled on the floor in front of the monitors, trying to stay near the fresh air. Tears slid down her face as she tried to take a deep breath. At this point, she prayed that if West was out there, he'd make it to her fast enough.

Charlee gasped as the men turned their guns on the animals. Human bullets could not kill shifters, she chanted over and over in her head. West had assured her that if he got shot, he would heal fine. But now that she was watching this horror unfold in front of her eyes, she didn't know if she wanted to observe it.

Seconds ticked by after Drago's announcement. West braced himself for the impact of bullets as the humans continued to hold their weapons steady. He didn't dare take his eyes off the human who dared point an automatic weapon in his direction. The silence was broken by the sound of text messages arriving to the humans' cell phones.

West knew immediately that the hit was officially cancelled. But some of the humans didn't lower their weapons immediately. The standoff continued for a brief moment before all the humans reluctantly lowered their weapons.

"Safe passage?" one of the humans asked.

"Safe passage," Drago repeated. "Go now and the animals will not attack."

Each shifter stayed in their positions as the humans slowly made their way away from the house and disappeared into the woods. West released the breath he didn't know he had been holding. His feline was upset that there would be no battle, but the human in him was relieved. His tiger would be satisfied once he laid eyes on Charlee and knew that she was safe.

His eyes turned to his cousin's house and the bottom of his stomach dropped. The fire's flames were moving through the house rapidly. Panic set in as he ran toward it, the thick smoke clouding the sky. He slowly transformed back to his human self, uncaring that he was naked.

"You can't go in there," Luka said, coming to stand next to him while hopping on one foot to throw on a pair of jogging pants.

"The hell I can't," he snapped, moving toward the building. Nothing and no one would stop him from entering the building. Shouting erupted behind them as the other shifters had transformed to their human forms and were rushing, trying to fight the fire.

West ran directly into the burning building. His eyes stung from the smoke. He knew that his cousin had a panic room and the girls would be stashed there. Coughs racked his body as he ran through the smoke filled home. His cousin had the room installed on the second floor a few years ago and had invited him to come see it. Thankfully, he remembered where the room was. The idea to shift crossed his mind. It would be quicker on all fours and he would be closer to the ground, but he wouldn't be able to get the door open without opposable thumbs.

The tiger in him growled and lent his strength, giving West a burst of energy as he came upon the stairs. He took the stairs two at a time as Luka shouted from behind him. He ignored his longtime friend. He had to get to her. The air grew scarce, causing his lungs to burn. If it was this hard to breathe outside the room, he couldn't even begin to imagine what it was like where Charlee and Malena were.

The hallway that greeted him was dark and thick with smoke. He blindly ran toward the direction of his cousin's office. Once he reached the open door, flames greeted him. He released a curse as he looked into the room and jumped back out of the way of the scorching flames as they grew.

"West! Here!" Luka shouted, arriving at his side with two fire extinguishers in his arms. "Not sure if these will help."

"Worth a try," West said, snatching one out of Luka's arm. He pulled the pin and aimed the fire extinguisher at the base of the flames. The white foam substance pushed back the flames, enough to allow West to enter the room with Luka behind him, using the other fire extinguisher. He made his way to the wall that hid the panic room.

He slammed his fist into the panel that hid the secured keypad. He remembered his cousin telling him the secret code that was the same emergency code that was used amongst all Rogavac's should they be in trouble. His fingers flew across the keypad and the light changed to green. His body grew tense as the steel door released a heavy groan and began to slide open.

It finally opened, revealing the small room. Malena and Charlee were huddled together on the floor in a corner.

"West!" Charlee gasped as he strode in toward her.

"Hey, baby," he murmured, collecting her in his arms.

"I got Malena," Luka announced, coming in the room behind him. "Go over to the balcony. The fire hasn't made it over there yet, and Drago and his men are waiting down below."

West's tiger seemed to settle down now that they had Charlee in their arms.

"I knew you would make it." Her voice was strained and ended on a squeak. His tiger didn't like seeing her this weak. As soon as they got her safely away from the burning house, he would put her on the first plane to the States.

"Of course I would. Don't talk," he murmured, stepping out onto the balcony. She closed her eyes and leaned her head against his chest. Now that the danger of her being hunted down was no longer there, West promised that he would take her home and lock them away for days so that he could have her to himself and fully assess her inch by inch to satisfy his tiger.

"Um, Luka?" Malena's scratchy voice appeared from behind them as he stepped out onto the balcony behind West.

"Yes, Malena?" Luka replied.

"Next time I need rescuing, you may want to step up your game. West, I see, knows how to rescue a woman." Her words were cut off by a string of coughs.

"Oh? And what's wrong with my technique?" Luka asked, shock registering in his voice.

West turned to them as Luka came to stand next to him.

"He's naked. Next time I need rescuing, you need to show up naked like your boy over there!"

TWENTY NINE

Two weeks later…

Charlee felt great for her first day back at the university. The past two weeks had been a whirlwind. Immediately after they left West's cousin's home, he had escorted her to the local hospital. After they were treated for smoke inhalation overnight, West had put them on a jet and flew them directly to the States, where he had the local leading physicians give her a thorough assessment. She had been given a clean bill of health. The gunshot wound had practically healed completely.

She sat back in her plush leather chair and sighed as she looked around her. She was a lucky girl. She knew it. Weston Rogavac was everything that she could imagine. Strong, sexy, protective, and alpha. What more could a girl ask for in a man? And he was able to shift into her favorite feline on the planet! He never failed to amaze her and she could honestly admit that she had fallen head over heels in love with him.

"Charlee?" Ellen's voice came over the speaker phone, causing her to jump slightly.

"Yes, Ellen?" she responded with her finger on the button.

"There's a reporter from the Cleveland Gazette on line one. Do you want to take it?"

Charlee plopped her head down on the desk with a groan. Since returning to the States, she had become a local celebrity. Her disappearance from the sanctuary had made international news. Of course the news had spun the story out of control. If she didn't know about it, she would have thought that she was the star of an action-packed suspense movie.

"No, I don't have anything to say," she answered, sitting back up. There was no way that she would talk to the press about her love life, or reliving the nightmare of getting shot and running from paid assassins. The press was like a pack of wild dogs, hunting for a story. Once word had gotten out that Weston Rogavac, one of the most eligible bachelors was in a committed relationship with her, the press had begun hounding her for the story.

Malena had told her that she heard talk of someone trying to make a movie based on the Siberia trip. An action-packed love story in the wilds of Siberia. It did sound good, but she shook her head at the thought. Who would want to play her in the story, a nerdy biologist who falls in love with a rich billionaire tiger shifter? She had to give it to them, the story did have a blockbuster ring to it.

"That's fine. I shall read off the same press release that Mr. Rogavac gave us." Ellen's voice floated through the air.

"Thanks, Ellen," Charlee said, punching a few keys on her keyboard. She still had a ton of work to do from the trip.

West had taken care of everything once they had returned. All of her belongings that were left back in Siberia had arrived at her home in perfect condition. All of their information that they had collected had been extremely valuable. The tagging of all the tigers had broken new ground in studying the animals. The real-time tracking was state-of-the-art, and had given them more information in the past few weeks than if spending six months in the wild.

Charlee's fingers flew across her keyboard as she became engrossed in her work. Jim and Alton had both emailed her their correlating research. They would be returning back to the States in the next week or so, and they would be able to put the finishing touches on the research to present to the Russian government. After they turned their information in, her and Dr. Zhang would be working on a new paper where they would publish their findings.

"Dr. Black, I'm sorry to bother you again, but your mother is on line one." Ellen's voice buzzed through the intercom.

"That's fine. I'll take this one." She smiled, grabbing the phone. "Hey, Mom."

"Hey baby. Why is your cell phone going straight to voicemail? I've been trying to call you for the past hour." Her mother's concerned voice greeted her ears. Joyce Black was not a woman to bite her tongue when it came to her children. Charlee felt a little guilty for shutting her cell phone off. She always answered her mother's calls. They were very close, and it was rare that they didn't speak at least once a day.

"You wouldn't believe the tenacity of the press. Somehow, they got a hold of my number and will not stop calling. I turned it off to try to get some work done today."

"Oh, my, that is crazy!" Joyce exclaimed. "Well, I won't keep you long. I was calling you because your father wanted you to bring your Weston to dinner again. I swear, that father of yours just loved Weston."

Since returning home, she had introduced West to her family. Her father and brother hit it off immediately with him. After the first dinner, the men had bonded and acted as if they were longtime buddies. It just warmed her heart that her family had quickly accepted West. Life was just too perfect right now. She couldn't be any happier with her and West's relationship. It had moved fast, but she didn't regret one part of their relationship.

"I'm sure he would love to come by the house," Charlee laughed. She wouldn't have to ask West. He had spoken nonstop about her father and knew the feeling was mutual.

"Good. Your father has went and purchased some new hunting thing and he wants to show it off."

Charlee rolled her eyes. Her father loved his hunting gear and could talk about it for days.

"Excuse me, Dr. Black—" Ellen's voice interrupted through the intercom.

"Hold on, Mom," Charlee said before pressing the button on her intercom. What could it be now? "Yes, Ellen?"

"You're needed in lecture hall twenty-four. Malena said that it's urgent."

"I have to go, Mom. I'll call you on my way home." She quickly ended the call. "I'm on my way," she assured Ellen.

She was unsure of what could be so urgent. She slid her heels back on, grabbed her keys and cell phone, and made her way out of her office. She didn't have any lectures today since it was to be a full day of work on her research. Her first lecture since returning to the university would be tomorrow.

The sounds of her heels clicking filled the air as she made her way toward her usual lecture hall. Within minutes, she arrived to find the lights out. She paused at the door, peering through the glass windows, and couldn't see anything. She opened the door, figuring that she just beat Malena and would wait for her to arrive.

She swiped the glass screen to her cell phone to call her and gasped as she turned on the light. The lecture hall was filled with thousands of long stemmed roses. She couldn't even see the floor due to the sea of red. Her eyes took in the beautiful flowers and began to fill with tears. A clear defined path was designed in the field of roses that led to the person who had come to mean so much to her.

West.

There he stood, looking sexy as ever in a dark suit, waiting for her, with a small smile etched on his face as he gazed at her. Her body on autopilot, seemed to float in his direction.

"Hey," she said as she arrived to stand in front of him.

"Hey," he repeated, reaching up to brush a strand of hair from her face. She leaned into his warm hand before he removed it and reached for her hand. He threaded their fingers together as he continued to stare down at her.

Her heart slammed against her chest as she gazed up at him, again, just amazed by him. She looked around the room in shock. She wiped away the tears that continued to flow down her face.

"What are you doing here?" she whispered, squeezing his hand tight. Her eyes grew wide as he knelt down before her and reached into his pocket. She became choked up with emotions as he pulled a small jewelry box from his jacket pocket. "Oh my God," she chanted over and over.

He chuckled as he opened the box, revealing an extremely large princess cut diamond. It was flawless, and Charlee was speechless.

"Charlee Black," he began. All joking disappeared from his face as he looked up at her. Her tongue was stuck to the roof of her mouth, so she nodded instead. "A tiger knows when he has found his mate.

When I first laid eyes on you, my tiger and I agreed on one thing. We wanted you, in every fashion known to humans and shifters."

"You have me," she murmured as the tears slowly continued to make their way down her face.

"I want it all. Charlee Black, will you do me the honor and become my wife and mate for life?"

Charlee knew that she didn't even have to think. She threw her body at him, wrapping her arms around him and squeezing him with all of her might. He barked out a laugh as she chanted yes, over and over.

There was no way that she would ever give him up. He wanted her for life, and he would get what he asked for. She just hoped that he and his tiger could handle her.

West stood next to the window in his downtown penthouse apartment and stared off into the night. Charlee snored softly behind him in the bed, exhausted after hours of lovemaking. His tiger was finally content that Charlee would be theirs. He was ecstatic that she had said yes to his proposal.

He could not exist without her. His tiger had deemed her his mate, and therefore, he would have done whatever he needed to do to have her. The past few weeks since they had returned to the States, West had Drago go back over everything that they knew about the trip. Something just wasn't right in regards to what went down. His initial gut reaction had been correct.

Dr. Skobo had been the person feeding the Bratva on the whereabouts of the group during their entire mission. That was how they were able to track their every move. West had turned in all of the intel that they had discovered over to the Russian government. Skobo had been arrested just that morning. With Charlee out of the way, he would have been able to take the lead on the research project and be named the lead researcher. The article that was being published to discuss their research was ground breaking and causing a stir in the animal wildlife community. With Charlee out of the way, he stood to make a name for himself.

The tiger in West growled slightly, wanting to go after the Russian biologist, but knew that their government would handle it. West would make sure of it. He would do whatever he needed to do to ensure that Charlee would remain safe. She was his, and this afternoon she agreed to forever with him.

"What are you doing?" she murmured. He glanced back at her and instantly felt his cock harden. Her sleepy eyes gazed at him, pulling at the strings to his heart. Her tussled look was downright sexy, and he found himself moving toward the bed. He had to have her again.

"Just thinking that it's time for me to mark you as mine," he growled, pulling the covers off her, revealing her sexy, naked curves. His claws broke through on his right hand, itching to mark her. One swipe of his claws and she would be his mate. The mark would let everyone know that she belonged to him.

"Make me yours, West," she moaned as he closed his lips around her beaded nipple. He settled in-between her legs, loving how she responded to him. It was time for her to become his forever in the way of shifters. Their human wedding would take place whenever she set the date. But for now, it was time for this tiger to mark his mate.

Letter To The Reader

Dear Reader,

Thank you for taking the time to read my book! I hope that you enjoyed reading the book as much as I enjoyed writing it. Please feel free to leave a review to let me know your thoughts. I love reading reviews from my readers. Even if you didn't like it, I would love to know why. Reviews can be left on Amazon, iBooks, B&N, Google, Kobo and even Goodreads!

Again, I just want to let you know that I am grateful for you and hope you will explore one of the other books I have written.

Love,
Ariel Marie

ABOUT THE AUTHOR

Ariel Marie is an author who loves the paranormal, action and hot steamy romance. She combines all three in each and every one of her stories. For as long as she can remember, she has loved vampires, shifters and every creature you can think of. This even rolls over into her favorite movies. She loves a good action packed thriller! Throw a touch of the supernatural world in it and she's hooked!

She grew up in Cleveland, Ohio where she currently resides with her husband and three beautiful children.

Sign up for Ariel Marie's Newsletter

Ariel puts this together to give her readers updates! Her subscribers are usually one of the first to learn about her releases, ARC signups and giveaways! Sign up for Ariel Marie's Book Junkie Fix:

http://eepurl.com/clg-H1

Also by Ariel Marie

An Erotic Vampire Series

Vampire Destiny

The Dark Shadows Series

Princess

Toma

Phaelyn

Teague

Adrian

Nicu

The Mirrored Prophecy Series

Power of the Fae

Fight for the Fae

Future of the Fae (TBD)

Stand Alone Book

Dani's Return

A Faery's Kiss

Fourteen Shades of F★cked Up: An Anthology

Her Warrior Dragon

CPSIA information can be obtained
at www.ICGtesting.com
Printed in the USA
FSHW021407260320
68491FS